KIWI SUNSET

In 1869, dismissed from her employment with Lady Howarth after being falsely accused of stealing, Mairin Houlihan emigrates to New Zealand. There she meets Marcus, the son of Lady Howarth, who had emigrated there to farm sheep. But later, despite her innocence, Mairin is held on remand on suspicion of murder. Marcus tries to help her — but with all the circumstantial evidence against her, how can he? If convicted she will hang. Who had committed this terrible murder?

MAUREEN STEPHENSON

KIWI SUNSET

Complete and Unabridged

LINFORD
Leicester

First published in Great Britain in 2006

First Linford Edition
published 2007

The moral right of the author
has been asserted

All the characters in this book are entirely fictitious
and have no relation to any living person.

British Library CIP Data

Stephenson, Maureen
    Kiwi sunset.—Large print ed.—
    Linford romance library
    1. British—New Zealand—Fiction
    2. New Zealand—History—19th century
    —Fiction 3. Love stories 4. Large type books
    I. Title
    823.9′14 [F]

    ISBN 978–1–84617–797–2

Published by
F. A. Thorpe (Publishing)
Anstey, Leicestershire
Set by Words & Graphics Ltd.
Anstey, Leicestershire
Printed and bound in Great Britain by
T. J. International Ltd., Padstow, Cornwall

This book is printed on acid-free paper

Grateful thanks to David, Julie, Bill and Sarah, for the research and help they have given me.

1

1869

It was a bright sunny spring morning when the great four masted sailing vessel the GEORGE WENTWORTH docked at Port Lyttelton, South Island, New Zealand. It had been a rough voyage with horrendous hurricanes in the South Atlantic but they had now finally arrived.

On the lower deck in one of the larger cabins Mrs Andrews, a grey haired middle aged woman, gathered together the women in her charge.

'May I have your attention? As you know, you were all carefully selected to join the agency set up by the British Government to help alleviate the shortage of women in New Zealand. You will all find work as cooks, nurses or maids, and can expect to receive proposals of marriage.'

Mairin Houlihan, a dark haired attractive girl stood on one side. She had been desperate to leave England, emigrate to New Zealand where she would start a new life, and of course see her dear sister Oonagh again who had emigrated there with her husband James and his parents five years ago. Now she was wondering had she made the right decision?

'I have an office in the main street of Port Lyttelton,' continued Mrs Andrews. 'It is over the grocer's store, and behind the building there is a bunk house where you will live until you meet your prospective employer.'

Mrs Andrews looked across at Mairin.

'Miss Houlihan, you are exempt from this rule because I understand you will be living with your sister at the Kiwi Accommodation House. I expect to see you at my office tomorrow morning at nine o'clock. Is that understood?'

'Yes Mrs Andrews,' replied Mairin dutifully.

Mrs Andrews then turned to the rest of the young women.

'It is now time to disembark.'

With Mrs Andrews leading the way they all moved out of the cabin in single file then climbed the ladder up onto the deck. Everyone was chattering and excited. They were a mixed bunch, some slim, some buxom, some plain, some pretty. They came from every social class, and many had unhappy stories to tell.

Mairin took a last look at the cabin that had been home for so long, at the bunks arranged along the walls, the long wooden table and benches down the centre of the cabin where all meals had been eaten, and the galley adjacent where they had all taken it in turn to cook their simple monotonous meals.

Mairin stepped onto the deck and joined her companions. Beyond the harbour rose a range of hills with half a dozen or so white weatherboard one storeyed houses scattered amongst them.

Mrs Andrews looked nostalgically at the landscape.

'I have relations who were amongst the first to emigrate to South Island,' she told them. 'That was in the 1850s. They had to live in tents.'

Mairin looked over the ship's rail. There were people still living in tents near the quayside with clothes drying on bushes and cooking their food over an open fire. Life was still hard. Mrs Andrews stepped down the gangway followed by her hopeful young women.

Mairin's friend Zillah was the last to leave.

'Good luck Zillah,' called Mairin.

'And good luck to you Mairin. You've been a good friend. I hope we meet again.'

As Zillah stepped down the gangway Mairin stood a moment at the rail frantically searching the small crowd at the quayside for a sight of her sister and her husband. She could not see them, it was probably because they had not received her letter. Letters could take as long as six months.

Mairin left the ship and started to climb the steep slope from the quayside. It felt strange to be on dry land again, and as she glanced around her everything seemed so English, then on closer inspection she saw a strange looking bird. It was small and dark with a large fantail, then she saw another one with a long orange beak. At the top of the steep slope was a tree with strange shaped leaves. She wondered if it was the cabbage tree Oonagh had told her about in her letters.

The Kiwi Accommodation House was easy to find being situated in the small main street not far from the quay. It was a one storeyed white weatherboard house similar to the other wooden houses in the street with a good view of Lyttelton harbour.

Entering by the main door Mairin walked into a small reception area where she immediately recognised Oonagh's father-in-law Mr Callcott. He was at a desk dealing with a crowd of prospective customers who had just disembarked from the GEORGE WENTWORTH.

Mairin was trying to attract his attention when suddenly the door behind him opened and there stood Oonagh's mother-in-law Mrs Callcott.

'Mairin, I can't believe it!'

She flung her arms around Mairin. Mr Callcott rose to his feet and shook her hand.

'You have just disembarked from the GEORGE WENTWORTH?' he asked.

'I certainly have. Where is Oonagh?'

'The baby was born yesterday,' Mrs Callcott told her. 'It's a girl and she is going to be called Hannah. Come with me and I'll take you to her.'

Mrs Callcott showed Mairin into a small room at the end of the corridor. Oonagh was lying asleep, a small newly born baby in her arms.

'Don't waken her,' Mairin whispered, but Oonagh's eyes were already open. She gazed at Mairin in disbelief.

'Am I dreaming?' she asked in a sleepy voice. 'Is it really you Mairin?'

Mairin bent and kissed her forehead.

'No, you are not dreaming. I really am here. Obviously you have not received my letter.'

'And you will not have received mine. Like to hold Hannah?'

Mairin took the little bundle into her arms. She certainly was a very pretty baby.

'You're lucky Oonagh. A good husband and a lovely baby.'

Mairin handed the baby back to Oonagh.

'What happened Mairin? You never gave any indication in your letters that you intended coming out here.'

As Oonagh spoke the bitter, humiliating memory flooded Mairin's mind.

'You were employed as a governess to Lady Howarth's niece,' continued Oonagh. 'What happened?'

Suddenly the tears came long and hard. Oonagh's arms went around her sister.

'Cry as long as you want Mairin. It will do you good.'

When Mairin's tears had subsided, she dried her eyes then looked at Oonagh.

'I was accused of stealing her ladyship's brooch, and given instant dismissal. I have never stolen anything in my life.'

'I know you haven't.'

'She tried to ruin my life.'

'I wonder why?' mused Oonagh. 'Her husband died a few years ago and her eldest son Joshua inherited the title and estate.'

'He was very domineering towards her,' continued Mairin. 'He employed me and it is her ladyship's duty to employ governesses.'

'Perhaps that was why it happened,' suggested Oonagh. 'An attempt to get her own way. You can't trust the Howarths,' Oonagh spoke in a firm voice. 'You must have known that. We lived in that village all our lives.' Then she gave her sister a quick look. 'Did you by any chance come out with the government agency? I mentioned it in one of my letters about the free passage.'

Mairin nodded.

'I'm registered as a cook, there is little demand for governesses. Oh Oonagh, it was the only way I could get out here. The vicar gave me a character reference. I told him I had been wrongly accused of stealing. He believed me.'

'A very kind man, even though our father was only a coal miner. Oh by the way, Lady Howarth's younger son Marcus, on his father's death, did not inherit anything, which is the custom, and he did what any sensible man would do and emigrated here. Land is cheap. He's got a sheep station on the Canterbury Plains. He stayed here once. We always have rooms to let. You have nothing to worry about.'

'I'm sure I haven't. By the way, where is James?'

'James works in Christchurch for a

Mr Hewlett. As soon as it is possible we will be joining him.'

The following morning Mairin put on her best gown, then pinning her hair neatly into a chignon, she put on her bonnet and cape then went to see Mrs Andrews as instructed.

Mrs Andrews sent her to meet a Mr Hunt who lived a few miles up the road. The moment Mairin saw him she did not like him; short, stout and bald, and she did not like the way he looked at her.

He showed her round the house and when he came to his bedroom he told Mairin they would be in the bed that night and if she pleased him he would wed her. He then told her he had to see a Maori man about some carving and would be back in an hour.

The moment he left Mairin could stand the place no longer. He was treating her like a whore. Leaving the house she took the road to Port Lyttelton, and went immediately to Mrs

Andrews' office. Mairin told her what had happened.

'I'm so sorry to hear this,' Mrs Andrews replied in a sympathetic voice. 'You must have been very disappointed. Anyway you are in luck. It just so happens I have a new gentleman on my list, a Mr Marcus Howarth. And there is a coincidence. He comes from Locksley in Warwickshire, the same village as yourself. He is looking for a bride and quite a catch, and you will know he is the brother of a baron.

'At the moment he is in Christchurch and will be calling in here tomorrow. I'll tell him to call at your sister's accommodation house. Shall we say half past two tomorrow afternoon?'

'Is it compulsory to meet Marcus Howarth?' Mairin asked in a quiet voice. She could feel a tension in her chest and sorry she had ever decided to join the agency.

'Miss Houlihan, it is obvious that I did not make myself plain. You must see at least two clients and if you refuse

11

there is a penalty to pay. Now are you willing to see Mr Marcus Howarth?'

Mairin had no alternative but to agree. She left the agency stunned at the news. Marcus Howarth! The younger son of that vicious evil woman. The following day at two thirty Mairin went to the reception room. Marcus Howarth was already there. His wide brimmed hat perched on the back of his head, an arrogant look on his handsome face.

'Good afternoon Miss Houlihan,' he began. 'I understand the agency has arranged for us to meet.'

Mairin gave him a hard look. 'I'm afraid . . . ' she began.

Suddenly the door opened and to Mairin's astonishment in walked Mr Hunt. He was drunk and lurched towards her.

'What are you doing here?' he asked looking at Marcus Howarth. 'Miss Houlihan and I have a lot to discuss.'

'We have nothing to discuss,' Mairin told him firmly.

Then Mr Hunt took a step towards her, his fists clenched, and from the expression on his face Mairin felt certain he was going to hit her.

'No,' she cried, taking a step back.

Then it all happened so quickly. Suddenly Mr Hunt lunged at Marcus Howarth with his fists, but he was too quick for him and punched Mr Hunt in the stomach. Mr Hunt bent double and collapsed on the floor. Marcus Howarth turned to Mairin.

'Do you know where he lives?'

'It's a house just a few miles up the road. I can see his pony and trap outside.'

'If I put him in his trap and drive him home, could you drive my waggon I have left outside? All you have to do is follow me.'

Mairin looked across at Mrs Callcott still seated at her desk who had been watching the confrontation between the two men with increasing astonishment.

'Will you tell Oonagh I have to help Mr Howarth?'

She nodded as Marcus Howarth picked up Mr Hunt, slung him over his shoulder and went out to the trap placing him in the passenger seat whilst Mairin followed climbing into the waggon positioned nearby. Then the two vehicles set off up the winding hill road out of Port Lyttelton.

Soon the house came into view by the side of the road. Marcus Howarth stopped the trap and helped Mr Hunt into the house. Mr Hunt now appeared conscious though weak on his legs.

They entered the house. Marcus Howarth reappeared some five minutes later, climbed into the driver's seat on the waggon and they set off.

'Thank you for helping me Mr Howarth,' Mairin told him in a grateful voice. 'I'd like to go back to the Kiwi now.'

'It's too late to turn back,' was the reply.

2

Mairin felt a tense nervousness in the pit of her stomach. She was trapped with a member of that obnoxious family. Turning she looked at Marcus Howarth as he sat beside her with his wide brimmed hat pulled well down on his head, a determined expression on his tough sunburnt face.

'You don't look happy,' he remarked. 'Thinking about Mr Hunt? His servant told me that is his name. Can you talk about it?'

'I'd rather not.'

They journeyed on for a while in silence. At length Marcus Howarth spoke.

'I feel there is something else troubling you besides the problem with Mr Hunt.'

'There is.'

'Well, tell me about it.' His voice now

had an edge of irritation in it.

'I come from Locksley.'

He gave her a slow smile.

'I thought I'd seen you somewhere before, back in the old country. Mrs Andrews told me your name is Houlihan,' he added thoughtfully, shaking his head. 'Your name is unfamiliar. Were you on visiting terms with Squire Easton's wife?'

'No,' replied Mairin, now an edge of irritation in her voice. 'No, I did not take afternoon tea with Mrs Easton. I had to work for my living.'

'Why are you getting so annoyed? Anyway, you didn't miss anything. Very boring family.'

They journeyed on for a while, Mairin staring straight ahead.

'When we first met this afternoon at the Kiwi,' Marcus Howarth continued, 'your opening remark to me was not encouraging. What were you about to tell me?'

Mairin took a deep breath.

'I was about to tell you that I had

decided not to be a bride for you.'

Marcus Howarth gave her an amused look.

'Why was that? You know nothing about me.'

'I know all about your family.'

'What have my brother and mother got to do with me?'

'Everything. You are all of the same blood.'

The amused smile was still on his lips.

'After the way your mother treated me,' continued Mairin, 'I couldn't possibly have anything to do with the Howarths.'

He gave Mairin a quick, apprehensive look.

'What did my mother do?'

'I was governess to your mother's orphaned niece. The young girl was making good progress. I felt I was doing a competent job. One night your mother called me to her dressing room and accused me of stealing her brooch.

'I have never stolen anything in my

life. I was appalled at the unjustness of it. She gave me instant dismissal. She tried to ruin my character. She never gave me a chance.'

'I am very sorry to hear this,' replied Marcus Howarth. 'Under the circumstances I think we had better forget the possibility of marriage between us. That is now out of the question. As I said it is too far to turn back to Lyttelton so I wish to make a proposition to you.'

'And what is that?' asked Mairin full of suspicion. He was after all a Howarth.

'How would you like to be my cook housekeeper for a limited period until I can get someone else?'

Mairin thought for a moment. It seemed the best solution to the problem.

'The answer is yes.'

'Good. I have a Maori woman who is an atrocious cook. Everything is burnt, but she is an excellent cleaner. She can remain to clean. Now as you were a governess I am speaking to an educated woman. Would you like to do my letter writing for me? I have a number of business interests in Christchurch and I feel it is time for me to be better organised. What do you think? I'll give you double the normal wage.'

Mairin paused a moment, not sure what to do.

'I'll take it.'

'I'm sure you won't regret it.'

Had she made the right decision thought Mairin desperately as the light started to fade. He was a Howarth after all and they were all the same, tough and cruel. Offering her double the normal wage. Why?

She gave him a quick worried glance.

Did she have duties other than cooking and letter writing? Mairin decided that if this was the case she would leave immediately.

'What are you worrying about?' The amused voice of Marcus Howarth broke into her thoughts.

'Nothing,' she lied. 'I presume we are on our way to your sheep station on the

Canterbury Plains?'

'Correct,' he replied with a whimsical smile. 'We will have to sleep tonight under the waggon. But don't worry you'll be safe. I'll be the perfect gentleman. Wrap yourself up in a blanket, and I'll waken you in the morning.'

He stopped the waggon. In the soft mellow light of sunset she could see the Canterbury Plains spread out before them, wide and green, covered in sheep. In fact she had never seen so many sheep in her life.

Soon Marcus Howarth had a good fire blazing. He produced a frying pan and started frying bacon, then from his knapsack he produced a loaf of bread.

Mairin pointed to the waggon loaded with furniture.

'Who is it for?' she asked.

'I felt it was time to improve the living quarters of my hired workers.'

Mairin felt so tired after they had eaten she rolled herself up in a blanket under the waggon and fell asleep almost immediately.

The following morning she was awake first, the thought in her mind that Marcus Howarth had actually saved her from a most unpleasant experience with that horrible Mr Hunt, and she should be grateful to him.

Raking the hot ashes, then pushing in a few dry twigs, she soon got a small fire burning. Then going down to the river she filled the kettle. In Marcus' knapsack she found bread and cheese. When he awoke he was presented with a hot cup of tea and a plate of bread and cheese.

He looked pleased.

'Lucky I met you,' he remarked with a smile. 'Even though you will not marry me. Mairin, don't associate me with my family. I know their faults. Why do you think I emigrated?'

Perhaps everything was going to be all right after all she thought as she cut another slice of bread. She had slept peacefully all night in her blanket, and

Marcus had behaved like the perfect gentleman as he had said he would. In fact he did not appear to be interested in her except that she was going to be his future cook housekeeper and letter writer.

After they had eaten everything was packed up and they were on their way. They forded another river, passed small settlements of two or three wattle and daub dwellings at cross roads, their roofs thatched. Wild flax and thistles growing by the roadside.

After journeying for several hours they turned off the main road onto a side lane and soon after that up a short drive to a white weatherboard house with a verandah running along the front, and nearby were two buildings which Mairin assumed would be the kitchen and the hired workers' huts.

A Maori woman came out to greet them with a welcoming smile. She was short and stout with black hair and dark eyes, wearing a skirt of flax reed. She was bare footed.

'Anahera, meet Miss Houlihan from England.'

Anahera gave Mairin an excited smile.

'You will live here?' she asked.

'Yes,' Mairin replied. 'I am going to do the cooking and write letters.'

'And you do all the cleaning,' added Marcus Howarth.

Mairin felt Anahera was pleased with the new arrangement.

A man came out of the hired workers hut. He was wearing a loin cloth and bare footed.

'Nga Hau, help me unload this furniture. And Anahera show Miss Houlihan one of the empty bedrooms and make up the bed. She spent last night under the waggon so I should think she is looking forward to a good night's sleep.'

Mairin left the men unloading and went into the house with Anahera. They walked into a comfortably furnished sitting room with the usual horse hair sofa and chairs. A wooden settle by the fire. The floor was polished wood with a few scattered rugs, and on a shelf nearby were a number of books.

Down a short corridor was Marcus' study. Nearby was his bedroom and a little further down the corridor the room where Mairin was to sleep.

It was a simple room, with just a small iron bedstead and a table and chair. The floor again was bare polished wood and at the small window hung simple cotton curtains.

Mairin settled into a daily routine of cooking and letter writing and Anahera did the cleaning, and as the days passed her detestation for Marcus gradually diminished. Every day he was kind and considerate, always the perfect gentleman. He didn't seem like a Howarth at all. A bond started to develop between them, a bond of friendship. It was extraordinary.

One morning at breakfast they had just sat down at the table. On the plates in front of them were bacon and fried bread.

'I'm afraid there aren't any eggs. Either someone is stealing them, or the hens have stopped laying.'

Marcus looked amused.

'Or the hens are hiding them. Mairin, I've got problems. One of the hired men is ill, another has cleared off, so I am short handed. Now I have a flock of ewes lambing for the first time. They are on the northern bank of the Wamakiri river and I need to go there in case any of them are in trouble. Will you come with me? I need an assistant. I have a quiet mare that would suit you.'

'I'll come,' Mairin told him.

They set off soon after breakfast with clean cord, some soap, and anything Marcus thought may be useful at a difficult birth.

For a while the going was fairly easy riding through scrub land, followed by wide stretches of good grazing, and all the time sheep, sheep everywhere.

At last they came to the Wamakiri river. They forded the river then rode slowly through the flock on the far bank. The sheep bleating continuously. They had lambed, and successfully except eight of them.

They dismounted and walked across to the ewes in distress. Marcus tied a cord round the head of one of the unborn lambs that was just protruding from the ewe. Mairin held the feet of the ewe whilst Marcus pulled. Slowly the lamb was born. Immediately she jumped to her feet and started feeding from the ewe.

They dealt with the other ewes in exactly the same way.

'We've been lucky,' Marcus observed as he remounted his horse. 'Only eight. Thanks for your help Mairin.'

They started the homeward trek. Soon it would be dark.

'I think it wise to stay overnight in the halfway hut,' announced Marcus. 'We have to ford a couple of rivers and one of them has quicksand.'

They found the halfway hut on the edge of a wood, a stream running past the door. Tying the horses to a nearby tree they opened the creaking door and peered inside. It was one room containing six bunks fitted to the walls, and an open fireplace.

Someone had thoughtfully left a pile of logs. They soon had a fire blazing and the billy can boiling. Mairin found a tea caddy filled with tea, and a knife in a drawer with which she cut the bread and cheese Anahera had thoughtfully given to her.

'Mr Howarth . . . ' Mairin began.

'Marcus,' he corrected her.

'Marcus, why are we so fortunate to have logs for the fire and tea in the caddy?'

He gave her a knowing smile.

'Not really. If any of my men ride this way they have instructions to call in the halfway hut and replenish logs and tea.'

It was now dark, and the interior of the hut lit by the light of the flickering fire gave it a warm cosy effect. They had finished their simple meal when

Marcus turned to her.

'I know very little about you Mairin, except you were employed by my mother as a governess. You are an attractive woman and still single.'

Mairin hesitated.

'Don't you want to talk about it?'

'Not really, but I suppose I must.' Mairin took a deep breath then spoke in a quiet voice. It was something she did not discuss with anyone, except Oonagh. 'I was going to marry a young man from Locksley, but he found someone he liked better.'

Mairin looked down into her lap, a look of embarrassment in her eyes.

'Happens all the time.' Marcus spoke in a soft gentle voice.

'He never said a word to me,' Mairin continued. 'I saw him with her by accident in the street. They were holding hands and the way they looked at each other I knew it was all over between us.'

There was silence for a moment, then Marcus spoke in a quiet voice.

'One of the reasons why I came to New Zealand.'

'Sorry to hear that.'

Gently Marcus took her hand in his.

'Are you tired?'

'I'm exhausted and my muscles are aching.'

'That's what I thought.'

He walked across to the first bunk then turned to her.

'Mairin, sometimes I feel I'd like to do more than just sheep rearing. Broaden my horizons shall we say.'

'Got any ideas?'

'None at the moment.'

He flung himself down on the bunk.

Mairin walked across to the bunk on the opposite side of the room and lay down. Suddenly she felt apprehensive. Just the two of them, a man and a woman, unmarried, sleeping in the same room! Could she trust him? She looked cautiously across at Marcus. He was facing the wall.

'Mairin!'

'Yes Marcus?'

Her heart was beating rapidly.

'Sleep well. We are up at first light.'

A few moments later he was sound asleep.

Mairin was not sure whether she was pleased or disappointed.

The following morning they were up at first light, washing in the stream, lighting the fire, boiling the billy can, making tea.

Marcus had little to say on the return journey except to thank her for her help. As she dismounted and entered the house she saw Anahera watching her from the kitchen window with a puzzled look on her round face.

Mairin now found herself looking forward to Marcus' return each evening. It was a strange feeling actually liking a Howarth. In the evenings she would listen to him for hours as he told her all about his problems in the early days when he was setting up the sheep station.

Sometimes he went away for days at a time. She never asked where he had been, considering it none of her business.

One evening after dinner instead of following his usual custom of going to his study Marcus went and stood before the fire gazing at her with such an intense look in his eyes it alarmed her.

'Anything wrong Marcus?'

'There is a lot wrong,' he replied, beckoning her.

Mairin walked across to him. He was a big strong man and towered over her. Then to her surprise his arms slowly entwined her, drawing her to him, then his lips gently kissed her neck, her ears and finally her mouth. She felt a shiver run through her. Then he was kissing her with the savagery of a hungry man, his hands clutching her breasts.

'This is a surprise,' she spoke in a low calm voice.

'A surprise?' he repeated. 'I thought you realised I am in love with you. Only God knows how I managed to control myself that night at the halfway hut.'

Suddenly there was a loud hammering at the door.

'Come quickly Mr Howarth. Your horse is sick,' called a masculine voice. 'We can't do anything with him.'

'I'm coming,' called Marcus in a sharp voice. Then, turning to Mairin added, 'I'm so sorry Mairin. I have to go.'

Giving her a quick kiss he hurried from the room. Mairin returned to her room, undressed and crept into bed. Marcus loved her! It was hard to believe, the brother of a baron loved her the daughter of a coal miner! He might ask her to marry him. It was a long time before she fell asleep.

The following morning she breakfasted alone. There was no sign of Marcus. What could have happened to him? Was he still with his sick horse?

Anahera entered the room.

'Where is the master?' Mairin enquired in a casual voice.

'He's gone to Christchurch. He had to see someone.'

It was mid morning. Mairin went to Marcus' study, mainly to tidy up the room and see if there was any work for her to do. A desk drawer was open. Just as she was about to close it she noticed a newspaper tucked inside.

She withdrew it with idle curiosity, turning to the page dealing with births, marriages, burials. It was a habit her mother always had, reading that particular page in their local newspaper.

Suddenly she saw it!

In the engagement column the announcement read:

'The engagement is announced between Mr. Marcus Howarth, late of Locksley Hall, Warwickshire, England, and Miss Georgiana Stuart-Erskine of Christchurch, New Zealand.'

3

Sitting at the open window, the fragrance from the kohuhu flowers drifting in, Mairin had rarely felt so unhappy. Marcus had never mentioned the name Georgiana Stuart Erskine, or any member of her family. She had brought this on herself, it was all of her own doing. Marcus had gone to the agency for a bride and she had refused him.

What a fool she had been! She was obviously relegated to the position of future mistress. Anahera had said the master had gone away for a few days. Was it to see Miss Georgiana Stuart Erskine?

Mairin started to pack her few possessions with a heavy heart. The stagecoach for Christchurch was twice a week and today was one of the days. She told Anahera to tell Marcus she had gone, then walking down the dirt track she was just in time for fifteen minutes later the stagecoach appeared round the bend in the road.

'Where are you going miss?' asked the driver.

'Christchurch,' Mairin told him. Oonagh had written giving her new address in Tyrone Street, one of the new streets recently built in Christchurch.

'Get inside. Pay me when we get there.'

Someone opened the door and Mairin stepped inside, seating herself between two large women.

Marcus had deceived her. She was nobody. No one of any account, and he obviously thought he could do whatever he liked with women such as her. Well, I've shown him today he can't thought Mairin, her spirits starting to rise.

It was early evening when they reached Christchurch. Mairin soon found Oonagh's house, and Oonagh was so pleased to see her sister.

'What happened?' she asked as she

led Mairin into the sitting room. 'I am surprised to see you in Christchurch.'

Mairin gave her a noncommittal reply. Later I will give her the details Mairin thought, but not now.

'How is James?' she asked as they sat down on the sofa.

'He's got a lot of problems. He won't discuss them with me. Anyway we are planning to go to Australia to join his parents. That news is confidential by the way. Now tell me what happened,' she insisted.

'He said he loved me.' Mairin's eyes filled with tears. 'Yesterday I read in the Christchurch newspaper the announcement of his engagement to . . . '

She could not continue. It was too humiliating.

Oonagh gave her a sad smile. 'Georgiana Stuart Erskine. I read it too. Forget that wretched man.'

The following morning Mairin placed an advertisement in the Christchurch newspaper seeking a governess post, and the day after she received a letter from a

Mr Hewlett of Worcester House wishing to see her that afternoon.

Oonagh was delighted.

'James works for Mr Hewlett. Remember I told you? He owns the South Island Loan and Savings Bank. You will have to hire a cab because Worcester House is about four miles from here.'

Mairin hailed a cab and set off. She must make a good impression, she must get the situation, she needed the money. She could not live off her sister and James indefinitely. She had a certain amount of pride.

Oonagh had been puzzled because the Hewletts did not have any children so if she got the situation who could she be teaching? Half an hour later the cab turned up the drive of Worcester House. It was the largest house Mairin had seen in New Zealand.

Built of white weatherboard, three storeys high with a grand looking verandah on the ground floor, and another one on the first floor with an ornamented staircase leading down to the garden. She judged the house to have at least twenty rooms.

Mairin asked the cabby to wait then climbed the steps that led to the impressive front door and rang the bell. A maid appeared smartly attired in her black gown and starched white apron.

'Yes?' she asked cheekily.

'Miss Houlihan,' Mairin told the maid. 'Mr Hewlett is expecting me.'

The maid led her into a wide entrance wood panelled hall, then along a corridor tapping on a door.

'Yes?' called an elderly masculine voice.

'Miss Houlihan to see you sir.'

'Show her in,' came the reply.

A well built, grey haired man in his fifties rose to his feet from behind a large desk. They shook hands.

'Please sit down Miss Houlihan and tell me about yourself. I was interested in your advertisement.'

Mairin sat down and started talking. To her surprise she felt completely at ease with the man. He spoke in a strong Midland accent. She told him about her teaching experience in Locksley.

'I do have to tell you,' she added in an embarrassed tone, 'I was unjustly dismissed from my last teaching post for a crime I had not committed.'

'What were you accused of?'

'Stealing her ladyship's brooch. I have never stolen anything in my life, and never will.'

He gave her a long hard penetrating look.

'Miss Houlihan, I will engage you. You are educated and I appreciate your honesty. There is something about you that tells me you are telling the truth. Now the appointment will only be for a few months. The problem is . . . ' He lowered his voice. 'First it is an extremely confidential matter, and what I am about to tell you must not be repeated.'

'You can rely on me Mr Hewlett.'

'Soon after I arrived in New Zealand in the 1850s,' Hewlett continued, 'I got married. My wife has been a good wife to me, but unfortunately she cannot read or write.

'Now I want you to teach her. You will understand Miss Houlihan now that I have prospered and moving in, shall we say, society, it is embarrassing to have a wife who is illiterate. I am of course just thinking of her.'

'Of course Mr Hewlett. I will do everything I can to help her.'

They discussed salary and agreed on a figure.

'It will of course be a residential post. Where are you living at the moment?'

'I'm living at my sister's. She is married to James Callcott.'

'James Callcott! Why didn't you say so before? James is one of my most loyal employees. When can you start? Tomorrow?'

'Certainly.'

'Right. I'll expect you at nine o'clock.'

On arrival at Tyrone Street Mairin found Oonagh and told her the good news. Next morning she took a cab to Worcester House. It was the same maid who opened the door.

'I hear you're going to work here,' she commented leading Mairin up the wide staircase and then along a corridor.

'She's all right Mrs Hewlett. Better than him.'

At the end of the corridor she opened a door and announced:

'Mrs Hewlett, Miss Houlihan is here.'

The maid closed the door and they were alone.

They were in a small cheerful room, the walls covered in a floral design wallpaper. There was a gate legged table near the window and armchairs around the iron fireplace.

A grey haired woman in a black gown sat in one of the armchairs, her hair drawn back into a neat bun on top of her head covered by a lace trimmed cap. She would have been an attractive woman when she was young, but all the beauty had gone and there was a sad look in her eyes.

Mrs Hewlett gave her a puzzled look.

'I don't remember my husband telling me you were coming.'

'He must have forgotten. I'm a teacher and Mr Hewlett wants me to teach you to read and write.'

A worried look appeared on the lady's face.

Mairin gave her an encouraging smile. She had to gain Mrs Hewlett's confidence, and sat down in a chair next to her.

'There is no hurry. We will take our time. How long have you been in New Zealand?' Mairin asked.

'About twenty years,' she replied. I was one of the early settlers in South Island,' she smiled remembering. 'I got a job in service. I was a maid of all trades. In those days you had to turn your hand to anything.'

'Were you involved in the Maori Wars?'

'Oh yes,' replied Mrs Hewlett with a certain amount of feeling. 'I was living in North Island,' she continued. 'But the situation became so dangerous we had to leave. We went to live on Stewart Island. It was a very worrying time.'

Mairin postponed the lesson and let Mrs Hewlett talk. It did her a great deal of good and she became relaxed. When she had finished telling Mairin about her early experiences she paused giving Mairin a look of concern.

'Are you going to give me lessons every day?'

'It would be the best idea.'

'Then the easiest for you is to stay overnight during the week and go home at the weekend.'

She rang the bell at her side. A few minutes later the maid appeared.

'Ena, show Miss Houlihan one of the spare bedrooms. There should be one on the second floor next to Mrs Quigley.' Mrs Hewlett turned to Mairin. 'Mrs Quigley is our house-keeper by the way. When that is done we'll have a light lunch in here.'

Mairin was shown a small pleasant

room with a wooden bedstead covered in a patchwork quilt, then taken to the kitchen of Worcester House which followed the colonial tradition of being a separate wooden hut on land at the rear of the house. Here Mairin was introduced to the housekeeper Mrs Quigley, a handsome dark haired woman in her mid forties the sort of person who has everything under control.

After lunch Mrs Hewlett had her first lesson. Mairin printed the alphabet on a sheet of paper and asked her to copy it in the exercise book she had brought with her.

For Mrs Hewlett it was a slow painful business. When she had completed the task Mairin suggested a rest from lessons for a short period and it was decided to take a walk round Mrs Hewlett's flower garden.

It was a blaze of colour and one of the most beautiful gardens Mairin had ever seen.

'This is the koru,' explained Mrs

Hewlett. 'Notice the long thin blue flowers. This is the kowhai.' She now pointed to a yellow bell like flower. 'And this is the tutukiwi, a green orchid type flower. This is the akatawhiwhi, and this is the kawharawhara.'

'How do you remember all these strange names?' Mairin asked. 'I would find it very difficult.'

Mrs Hewlett smiled.

'The answer is I love flowers. If you love something, it is easy.'

They returned to the house.

'You have the most beautiful garden I have ever seen,' Mairin told her.

'I think you and I are going to be friends.'

And so Mrs Hewlett and Mairin fell into a pleasant routine. Each morning they had breakfast together in Mrs Hewlett's private sitting room. In the evenings they dined in the main dining room on the ground floor. Mr Hewlett was rarely at home. He seemed to spend most of his time in Christchurch.

Mrs Hewlett started to make

progress, very slowly and each day there was a slight improvement. Mairin gave her lessons in reading and writing for one hour in the morning and one hour in the afternoon. She did not want to make the lady's studies too intense and tire her.

At night Mairin would lie in her little bed on the second floor and a feeling of intense loneliness would sweep over her. When she thought of Marcus the ache in her heart would become almost unbearable. How could he have deceived her so? How could he have treated her so badly?

It had been arranged that she would have Sundays off, leaving Worcester House on Saturday afternoon to spend the weekend with her sister.

At the end of the first week on Saturday afternoon Mrs Hewlett had just completed her lessons for the day, when Ena knocked at the door and told her the master had just arrived from Christchurch and wanted to see Mairin.

Mairin found Mr Hewlett on the

ground floor in the main drawing room, a room Mairin had not entered before. It was very large and wood panelled with paintings of New Zealand landscapes in large gold frames hung around the room.

Mr Hewlett was reclining in a leather armchair smoking a cigar looking very pleased with himself.

'Now Miss Houlihan, what kind of a week have you had with my wife?'

'A good week Mr Hewlett. She is making progress.'

'Anything you require please let me know. I am always here on Saturday afternoons.'

When Mairin returned to Mrs Hewlett's sitting room the lady gave her an anxious look.

'What did you say to him?' she asked in a nervous voice.

'I told him you are making good progress, and you are.'

'You are very kind Miss Houlihan. I suppose you are now off to your sister's. Ask Gilbert the butler to take you in the trap. See you on Sunday and don't be late,' she called as Mairin left the room.

Half an hour later Mairin was in the trap driven by Gilbert the butler and on her way to Christchurch. So far being tutor to Mrs Hewlett was turning out to be a pleasant occupation, and the pay was good.

Gilbert stopped outside Oonagh's house. As much as Mairin liked her new situation she was happy to return to Oonagh's. The maid showed her through to the dining room where dinner was about to be served.

'How did you get on at Worcester House?' asked James as Mairin sat down at the table.

'Very well I am pleased to say. Everything went smoothly. I like Mrs Hewlett.'

James and Oonagh had no comment to make.

'I understand Mr Hewlett owns the South Island Loan and Savings Bank,' Mairin commented as the maid brought in the dessert.

'And doing very nicely I may add,' smiled James. 'Best move I ever made working for him. Anyway, I have told my parents we will join them in Sydney. There is a good future there.'

The conversation then turned to more general topics and when the meal finished James turned to Mairin.

'Oh by the way Mairin, I have some news for you. Remember your ex-employer Marcus Howarth?'

How could she forget him.

'I remember him.' Mairin tried to sound casual but her voice was tense.

'He's been made a director of the bank. He's invested quite a large amount in the bank,' James continued. 'Apart from that it is beneficial to have the brother of an English lord on the board of directors.'

Mairin could feel a tension gathering within herself. If Marcus Howarth had been made a director of her employer's bank, there was a possibility that they might meet at Worcester House.

Mairin had thought she would never

see him again. She hadn't given a thought to the small population of British immigrants living in South Island and consequently were bound to be a closely knit society.

'And Mr Hewlett has invited him to dinner one evening next week,' continued James. 'At Worcester House of course. I think it is Wednesday evening.'

Then James turned to Mairin.

'You're looking worried Mairin. What is the matter? Did you part on bad terms from Mr Howarth?'

Mairin gave him a faint smile. The matter was too private, too embarrassing to discuss with her brother-in-law.

On Sunday evening when she returned to Worcester House her apprehension returned. She made a firm resolution that on Wednesday evening she would keep to her room and go nowhere near the dining room, but at the same time she felt sad.

Mairin had grown to like Marcus Howarth more than she had realised. She missed his company. The evenings now seemed long and empty without him. Did he miss her? Obviously not.

Mairin went along to Mrs Hewlett's sitting room. She felt so frustrated with life. Would it always be like this? Paying the price for making the wrong decision.

Mrs Hewlett was alone, sat at the table knitting. Mairin took off her bonnet and cape and sat down opposite the lady. Mrs Hewlett was frowning.

'Mr Hewlett has invited one of his new directors to dinner on Wednesday evening and has asked me to attend. Mairin, I'm not used to mixing with such company. His brother is a baron.

'I'm afraid of making a fool of myself, saying something stupid. I was only ever a domestic servant, and so was my mother. My father was a fisherman. How can I talk on equal terms with this Mr Howarth?'

'Mrs Hewlett you can,' Mairin insisted. 'You can do it. You are as good as him. Remember you are the wife of Mr Hewlett, one of the leading citizens of Christchurch.'

'You're very kind, but I'm dreading it.'

'Wear your best gown,' Mairin advised. 'Being well dressed will help your self confidence, and I could rearrange your hair into a new style, that is if you agree.'

Mrs Hewlett nodded her head.

'Mairin, I want you to join us for dinner on Wednesday evening. I would feel so much better if you were there. You make me feel confident.'

The prospect of spending the evening in the company of Marcus made her feel deeply unhappy. It was opening up an old wound. He was bound to demand an explanation regarding her disappearance from his household. There could be angry exchanges.

'Mr Hewlett doesn't want me there,' Mairin protested with a feeling of desperation. 'How would he explain my presence? He has told me teaching you to read and write is highly confidential.'

'He will introduce you as my

companion. I can get my own way sometimes,' she added with a smile. 'Now time we had some lunch.'

And so on Wednesday evening Mairin dressed for dinner putting on her black and white muslin gown. It was grossly out of fashion, one that Oonagh had given her many years ago, but she was grateful to her. Then Mairin went along to Mrs Hewlett's bedroom dreading the evening that lay ahead.

She helped the lady dress. She rearranged her hair, making the style more attractive. Mrs Hewlett looked at herself in the mirror and felt pleased with the result. Then going down the stairs they went to the drawing room where Mr Hewlett and Marcus were awaiting them.

Both men looked surprised as they entered the room, Mr Hewlett at his wife's changed appearance and Marcus at Mairin's presence.

'There is no need for introductions,' said Mr Hewlett giving Mairin a welcoming smile. 'I understand Mr

Howarth was your last employer Miss Houlihan.'

There was an angry look in Marcus' eyes, a look of accusation. He made her feel she had done something that was unforgivable.

'Yes, I was her last employer, but I warn you Mr Hewlett she can be fickle.'

'I'm sorry to hear that.' Mr Hewlett looked amused, he was not taking the remark seriously. 'Now let's go into dinner.'

Mr Hewlett took his wife's arm and Mairin walked at Marcus' side.

'You didn't have the courtesy to leave me a note,' he whispered.

'I told Anahera to tell you.'

'Nice getting it second hand from a servant,' he replied sarcastically. 'Anyway, what was it all about?'

Their private conversation had to cease as they had now entered the dining room. Mairin sat at the circular mahogany table with Marcus on her left, Mr Hewlett on her right and Mrs Hewlett seated across the table.

The conversation seemed to be mainly about the poor condition of the roads, that immigration had to increase, and all the time Mairin could feel Marcus' hard angry eyes upon her. Finally the meal came to an end and Mrs Hewlett asked to be excused she was feeling tired and Mairin accompanied her back to her rooms.

In her dressing room Mairin helped Mrs Hewlett undress. Finally she was in her nightgown and in her bed.

'Mr Hewlett is a poor sleeper,' Mrs Hewlett informed Mairin. 'Sometimes he gets up in the night to read his company reports. So he decided it was better if he had his own room and did not disturb me.

'He is a kind and considerate man. The best thing that ever happened to me was marrying him. Tonight was a great success and it was all due to you.'

'Why me?' asked Mairin in surprise.

'It was just you being there.'

Mairin left the room and went down the corridor, suddenly remembering she had left her evening bag in the dining room.

As soon as she entered the room she realised her mistake. She should have gone to the kitchen and asked Ena the maid to get it for her. Marcus was there, standing before the fireplace.

He was alone. His eyes looked at her hard and accusingly.

'How could you do it?' His voice was low.

Now Mairin felt angry.

'How could I do it?' she retorted sharply. Then lowering her voice added: 'Making love to me and all the time . . . '

The thought of that announcement of his engagement made her feel she was going to choke. She felt a lump rise in her throat. Then just at that moment she heard Mr Hewlett's step as he returned to the drawing room.

'Miss Houlihan, I thought you had gone to bed.'

'I came back to look for my evening bag.'

Picking it up from a nearby chair Mr Hewlett handed the bag to her. 'Good night Miss Houlihan.'

'Good night Mr Hewlett.' Then turning to Marcus, her face expressionless, her voice low, 'Good night Mr Howarth.'

She left the room without a backward glance.

In her room on the second floor Mairin undressed, then flung herself down on the bed. There was a faint moonlight from a new moon. She had been so content here she thought sadly. Now she felt her heart was going to break.

As Marcus was now a director of Mr Hewlett's bank there would be regular dinner engagements, and Mrs Hewlett would be sure to ask her to accompany her. Life here was going to become intolerable.

She had to leave. Find a new situation. Her pillow was wet with tears that night.

The following morning she dressed

with a feeling of low spirits, praying that Marcus had left last night for his Christchurch hotel and was now on his way back to his sheep station.

She went first to the kitchen to collect the breakfast tray. Mrs Quigley the housekeeper, and Ena the maid had been busy until late last night and Mairin felt it was her duty to give a helping hand.

Mairin opened the door of the kitchen hut. Mrs Quigley and Ena were there, but to her surprise she saw a new member of the kitchen staff, a Maori woman. She was young with long black curly hair, brown eyes, and a pleasing smile, dressed in the usual traditional Maori costume of a long flax reed skirt, a red band threaded through her hair, and barefooted. She was stirring porridge at the fire.

'This is Aroha,' introduced Mrs Quigley. 'Our new kitchen maid. This is Miss Houlihan, your mistress's companion.'

Aroha turned and smiled at Mairin,

Mairin smiled back.

'Mrs Hewlett also told me to take on a Maori odd job man,' Mrs Quigley continued. 'His main duty will be logs for the fires. Bit premature I thought considering it is now summer. She could have waited until the beginning of autumn. Then we would really need him.'

Mrs Quigley made the tea.

'Aroha, if you do as you are told, you'll fit in well here. Now why don't you tell Miss Houlihan one of your stories. She's a great story teller.'

Aroha took the pan of porridge off the fire.

'I hope you like it,' she said shyly. 'It is a story my mother always told.'

'In the beginning of the start of time the Sky Father lay in the arms of the Earth Mother with the gods, their children between them.

'They had many children and the space between the Sky Father and the Earth Mother became so cramped the children grew restless, longing for freedom. They wanted to feel the wind blowing, feel the sun warming them.

'Gradually the children pushed their parents apart and the Sky Father never saw his wife the Earth Mother again. When it rains it is the Sky Father weeping for his lost wife, and when the land is covered in silver mist it is the Earth Mother weeping for her lost husband.'

'Delightful,' Mairin told her. 'But very sad.'

Mairin picked up the tray and as she left the room she saw the Maori odd job man, dressed only in his loin cloth and bare feet enter the kitchen from the outside door. He gave her a happy smile. Mairin was getting a good impression of Maori people.

Each day Mairin was busy as Mrs Hewlett's teacher and in the evenings she started making herself a new gown cut from a gown Mrs Hewlett did not want. Mairin was conscious of the fact she had very little money and must save every penny she could earn. A time would come when her services would not be required. Apart from that she wanted to keep herself well occupied so that she did not have time to think of Marcus. It would only make her very unhappy.

And so the week past and on Saturday afternoon Gilbert drove her to Oonagh's house. There she spent a pleasant weekend and on Sunday evening returned to Worcester House.

The moment she entered the house she saw the letter. It was from Marcus.

My dear Mairin,

It was such a relief to meet you at Worcester House. I have been extremely worried about you. I can only assume you left me so suddenly because you had read the announcement of my engagement. I had intended discussing the matter with you. It has always been understood in my family that I would wed my second cousin Georgiana. I have no interest in the lady and made it plain to my mother who ignored me and went ahead with the announcement in the London and New Zealand newspapers.

If I break off the engagement Georgiana will sue me for breach of promise. She would ruin me. This is a problem I am determined to resolve. Come back to me Mairin. I love you.

Marcus.

4

Mairin was in a strange mood, both happy and sad.

Happy because Marcus still loved her and sad because nothing could come of this doomed relationship. Then she thought of the cruel way his mother, Lady Howarth, had treated her at Locksley and she was filled with an anger so intense she went up to her room immediately and began writing:

Dear Marcus,

I was surprised to learn that the announcement of your engagement to Miss Georgiana Stuart Erskine was against your wishes. Surely you have better control over your mother.

I also wish to inform you there can be no future relationship of any kind between us.

Mairin.

Taking the letter downstairs to the hall she placed it on the table with the other letters Gilbert would be posting in the morning. It was one of his duties to take any letters for posting to the post office. Returning upstairs Mairin paused at the door of Mrs Hewlett's sitting room and knocked.

'Come in,' she called.

Mrs Hewlett was sat by the empty fireplace knitting.

'Please do not think I am intruding into your private life.' Mrs Hewlett had a worried look. 'I think you have just received a letter from Mr Howarth. It was delivered by hand and Gilbert learnt who the sender was. He always talks to anyone who delivers letters.

'Now don't do anything foolish. Mr Howarth is an attractive man, owns a large sheep station and I understand from Mr Hewlett his engagement to Miss Stuart Erskine has just been announced.'

She gave Mairin a gentle smile.

'I'm not going to do anything

foolish,' Mairin replied.

'I'm so glad to hear it. It's just that I don't want you to spoil your life.'

'Of course not.'

'I'm going to bed early tonight. I have rather overdone it in the garden today.'

Mairin helped Mrs Hewlett to her bedroom which led out of the sitting room. Bidding her good night Mairin then returned to her room. She was not going to do anything foolish, much as she was longing to. She sat by the window looking out onto the dark silhouette of the kowhai trees. In daylight they looked so beautiful with their yellow bell-like flowers.

Suddenly Mairin had never felt so lonely. Now she was beginning to regret writing the letter. Why hadn't she paused and thought, instead of acting on a sudden impulse. She had done this all her life.

She wanted to return to Marcus, whatever the circumstances, she would at least be with the man she loved, for now she was certain she loved him.

The following morning after breakfast Mairin and Mrs Hewlett went for a walk in the garden before starting lessons. It was when they were returning to the house that Mrs Hewlett suddenly remembered.

'This coming Sunday Mr Hewlett and I are giving a dinner party. You are of course invited. And your sister and her husband Mr Callcott are also invited. Mr Callcott is an invaluable assistant to my husband,' she added with a smile.

Mr Hewlett is planning many more dinner parties,' Mrs Hewlett continued. 'So that I can meet more people. He is such a kind, thoughtful man.'

They went indoors, proceeded with a writing lesson, and all the time Mairin was wondering if Marcus would be invited. It would be agony to sit through another dinner party with his angry eyes upon her.

Next morning Mairin went as usual to the kitchen hut to collect the breakfast tray. The door opened and Aroha entered, her bare feet pattering across the wooden floor, then she stood silently at the table smiling at Mairin. Mairin felt she wanted to ask her something but was too shy to do so.

'What does Aroha want of me?' Mairin asked turning to Mrs Quigley.

'She wants to tell you another Maori story.'

'Aroha, I'd love to hear one.'

Aroha pleased at the invitation began: 'This is the story of the woman in the moon.'

When she had finished Mairin complimented her.

'Thank you Aroha. What an entertaining tale. By the way we tell stories about the man in the moon,' Mairin added laughingly.

'No,' Aroha replied firmly. 'It is the woman in the moon.'

Mairin took the breakfast tray to Mrs Hewlett's sitting room. After breakfast they went for a walk in the garden. Now that summer was here many of the flowers were in bloom. On the edge of the path was a beautiful large white flower that had just blossomed.

'What is that flower called?' Mairin asked.

'That is the New Zealand clematis,' she told her. 'One day someone will have to list all the New Zealand flowers and trees. And one day someone will have to write the history of New Zealand. My husband can tell you a lot about that. I know it all started with the Treaty Of Waitangi in 1840 giving New Zealand to Britain. You ought to get him talking about it.'

They returned to the house and commenced a reading lesson. Mrs Hewlett was improving tremendously. Mairin told her so. Mrs Hewlett looked pleased.

'It's all due to you.'

'It was Mr Hewlett's idea to employ me,' Mairin reminded her. 'He should get some credit.'

On Friday morning Mrs Hewlett sent Mairin to the kitchen to discuss with

Mrs Quigley the menu for the forth-coming week. She found the good woman in a worried state pouring over her recipe book.

'It's this dinner party on Sunday night, and I am looking for something really special. Mr Patrick O'Brien is coming.'

'Who is he?'

'One of the top lawyers in Christchurch, a widower I believe with a small son.'

'Why is this lawyer coming?'

'He does a lot of work for Mr Hewlett in connection with the bank.'

Mairin returned to Mrs Hewlett's sitting room.

'Mairin, I forgot to tell you Mr Callcott is coming this morning to discuss making my will. It appears that Mr Hewlett has made his and naturally it is right and proper that I make mine. I'm not getting any younger,' she added with a smile.

'Anyway Mr Hewlett thinks Mr Callcott should discuss the will with me first, then this afternoon he will accompany me into Christchurch to see Mr Patrick O'Brien and make my will.'

'Shall I spend the morning in my room?' Mairin asked politely. 'Discussing your will with Mr Callcott is a private affair.'

'No Mairin. You stay here. There is nothing I have to say to Mr Callcott that cannot be said in your presence.'

An hour later James arrived. The two of them sat down at the table and Mairin sat at the window sewing. It appeared that Mrs Hewlett wanted to leave her money and possessions to her husband.

'What do you want to do with your jewellery Mrs Hewlett?' James asked.

Mrs Hewlett gave a big sigh.

'I haven't got a daughter to leave it to,' she said sadly. 'And some of the pieces are very valuable. I leave it all to my husband. He'll know what to do with it, except of course the butterfly brooch.'

70

Mrs Hewlett turned and looked at Mairin.

'Mairin, I want you to have it.'

'You are so generous Mrs Hewlett.'

'It's the least I can do after what you have done for me.'

James then accompanied Mrs Hewlett and Mairin to the offices of Mr Patrick O'Brien of Christchurch. Mairin was introduced to him, a man in his thirties, pleasant looking.

After the will had been written they returned to Worcester House. Mrs Hewlett asked James to accompany her to her sitting room. She rang the bell and a few minutes later Ena appeared with a tray of afternoon tea.

It was when they had finished tea that James asked to see Mrs Hewlett's jewellery.

'I am concerned about its safety. I understand from Mr Hewlett that you do not have a safe.'

'I don't feel the need for one. The house staff are all trustworthy people.'

'May I see where you keep it?'

'I keep my jewellery in the bedroom. Come this way.' Mrs Hewlett led James into her bedroom.

'Come in here Mairin,' Mrs Hewlett called. 'I want to show you the butterfly brooch.'

Mairin followed them into the room. Mrs Hewlett went to her bedside cupboard and opened it. Inside was a large carved wooden box. She brought it out, placed it on the bed and opened the lid.

Mairin had never seen such a magnificent display of jewellery. There was an amethyst necklace with an amethyst cross hanging from it. There was a large circular diamond brooch, ruby ear rings, a ruby and pearl necklace.

There was a sapphire and diamond ring, a gold bracelet, a diamond bracelet, a sapphire necklace, a diamond necklace. It was like looking at the jewellery collection of a duchess.

Mrs Hewlett then pointed out to Mairin the butterfly brooch she wanted her to have. It was most attractive studded with diamonds and emeralds.

'You are so kind Mrs Hewlett,' Mairin told her. 'I am overwhelmed by your generosity. I've never had anything valuable in my life.'

Mrs Hewlett put her arm around Mairin's shoulder.

'You are the daughter I never had. You have done so much for me. You have made me a confident, contented woman. The brooch is the least I could do for you.'

James was looking worried.

'Mrs Hewlett, as I have already said I am most concerned about the safety of your jewellery. This wooden box hasn't even got a lock on it. The jewellery must be kept in a safe.'

'My jewellery has always been stored in this bedside cupboard, and nothing has ever happened. You are worrying unnecessarily.'

She gave him a weary smile, and started to leave the room. James put his hand on her arm.

'I am not Mrs Hewlett,' James insisted. 'Now that the Maori wars are over large numbers of immigrants are pouring into this country. Some of them could be desperate people.'

Mrs Hewlett turned pale.

'You can't be serious Mr Callcott.'

'Unfortunately I am,' James replied with a sad smile. 'I heard only the other day of a house broken into in Christchurch and all the valuables stolen. In the early years only respectable people emigrated here. Do you remember?'

'I do,' replied Mrs Hewlett.

They returned to her sitting room.

'Mr Callcott, will you arrange for me to have a safe? A small one will be sufficient for my needs.'

'I will arrange it. Leave it to me. Now I must return to Christchurch.'

And with that he left the room. Mrs Hewlett gave Mairin a weary smile.

'He's such an earnest young man and means well. And Mr Hewlett thinks very highly of him. But I can't help thinking he is exaggerating the situation. Mr Hewlett and I have been married all these years and nothing has ever been stolen. Anyway, I agreed to please him.'

They sat down in the armchairs by the window, and Mairin gave Mrs Hewlett a short lesson in reading and writing. She was always conscious of the fact she must not overtire the lady. This was followed by weeding the flower beds.

They retraced their steps back to the house.

'Go up to my sitting room Mairin,' Mrs Hewlett instructed her. 'I want to speak to Mrs Quigley about Sunday's menu.'

She turned and walked away down the corridor. Mairin went upstairs, and as she opened the door of Mrs Hewlett's sitting room, she thought she heard a sound coming from her bedroom.

'Who is there?' she called, but there was no answer.

Mairin opened the door of Mrs Hewlett's bedroom and to her surprise found the Maori odd job man standing in the centre of the room.

'What are you doing here?' Mairin demanded, feeling annoyed.

'I bring logs for the fire,' he replied, his large dark eyes looking at her in a shifty manner.

'But it is summer, and the weather is hot. We do not need a fire.'

He did not answer and left the room. How extraordinary she thought, bringing logs into Mrs Hewlett's bedroom to light a fire and the weather was stiflingly hot. She set out the text books for the next lesson and a few minutes later Mrs Hewlett arrived.

'Mairin, something has happened. I can tell from the look in your eyes.'

'I found the Maori odd job man in your bedroom. He had just brought in a pile of logs. I don't understand it. It is now summer and it is hot. I think you ought to see your jewellery is still there.'

Mrs Hewlett went into her bedroom

looking most concerned. Mairin followed her. Mrs Hewlett opened her bedside cupboard. The jewellery was still there.

'Mairin, you are worrying about nothing,' she reprimanded her.

'Of course I am,' Mairin replied with a relaxed smile.

They started the lesson and the matter was forgotten, and the following morning Mairin could not help raising the matter of the Maori odd job man with Mrs Quigley.

'I'll see it doesn't happen again,' she told Mairin.

'Sometimes I wonder if he's all there.' She tapped her forehead with her finger.

On Saturday afternoon Mairin was just about to leave with Gilbert for her short weekend break with Oonagh when a horse and cart appeared on the drive, stopping at the main front door. The notice on the side of the cart read:

HANCOCK SECOND HAND FURNITURE.
LIMERICK STREET
CHRISTCHURCH

'Mrs Hewlett in?' asked the driver, a rough looking man with a long grey beard.

'Yes she is,' Mairin replied feeling puzzled. Mrs Hewlett had not mentioned a Mr Hancock would be calling on her.

'Is she expecting you?'

'Not really. Mr Hewlett wrote to me a long time ago in the winter. Said his wife had some old furniture she did not want. I didn't call earlier in the year because I've been ill.'

Mairin asked Gilbert to wait for her and took the man up to Mrs Hewlett's sitting room.

'Mrs Hewlett,' Mairin called as she opened the door. 'Mr Hancock is here about some furniture you want to sell.'

They entered the room.

'Good day to you Mr Hancock.' Mrs

Hewlett greeted him courteously. 'There are two pieces of furniture in my bedroom I want to sell.'

She showed Mr Hancock into her bedroom. Mairin followed. 'There Mr Hancock.' She pointed to an armchair and a small rickety table.

'I'm sorry they are so shabby. Would you like them?'

The man nodded.

'I'll sell them without any trouble.'

'Mrs Hewlett, I'll have to leave you. Gilbert's waiting,' Mairin butted in.

Mrs Hewlett accompanied her out of the bedroom and into the sitting room leaving Mr Hancock alone in the bedroom. She talked for several minutes about the forthcoming dinner party.

'I'm afraid I will have to leave you,' apologised Mairin. 'I don't want to arrive late at Oonagh's.'

'Of course you don't,' replied Mrs Hewlett. 'Oh by the way, my husband wanted to invite Marcus Howarth but I told him Mrs Quigley and Ena already have enough to do coping with six for dinner.

'Now don't forget. On Sunday evening be here at seven o'clock sharp. We dine early as you know. And I'm so pleased Patrick O'Brien can come,' she added giving Mairin a sharp look.

Mairin left the room, hurried down the stairs, and into the waiting trap relieved that Marcus would not be coming to the dinner party.

'Sorry Gilbert but I had to deal with Mr Hancock. Mrs Hewlett is selling off some of her old furniture,' Mairin told him as they set off down the drive.

'Why?' laughed Gilbert. 'Is she hard up?'

'I shouldn't think so,' Mairin smiled back.

When Mairin arrived Oonagh was sat alone in the sitting room.

'Where's James?' she asked sitting next to her sister on the sofa.

'Only God knows,' Oonagh replied in a weary voice.

'What is the problem?'

'We are in serious financial difficulties.'

'How serious?'

'Very serious,' she replied. 'We have borrowed money from the bank and we can't pay back.'

'Which bank?'

'Mr Hewlett's. When we first took out the loan the agreement was to pay back in three years. Now Mr Hewlett wants the money back in four months.'

'Is it a lot of money?'

Oonagh nodded.

'Why did he change the terms of the agreement?'

'I don't know,' she replied in a depressed voice.

A few minutes later James arrived, looking worried. They went into the dining room and sat down at the table.

'Sorry I'm late but there is a lot of work at the moment.'

Then James turned to Mairin with a smile on his lips.

'Marcus Howarth is coming to dinner tomorrow night at Worcester

House. And I hear Patrick O'Brien has also been invited. Should be quite an entertaining evening. Marcus Howarth will be too outspoken for Patrick O'Brien's taste.'

Mairin's heart sank. It was going to be a disastrous evening. Marcus had become engaged to someone he did not want, and if he breaks off the engagement he will be taken to court and sued. And Mairin had a feeling Mrs Hewlett was trying to match her with Patrick O'Brien.

That night sleep did not come. Mairin tossed and turned trying to think of some reason why she should be absent from the dinner party but could think of none.

The following day they set off in the early evening in Oonagh and James' phaeton. Mairin was tense, dreading the evening.

When they arrived at Worcester House Gilbert opened the front door and showed them into the drawing room where Mr and Mrs Hewlett,

Patrick O'Brien and Marcus were already waiting.

Oonagh was introduced to Patrick O'Brien and Marcus' intense blue eyes gave Mairin a hard look, his mouth set in a firm line. They stood talking for a few minutes, James directing his conversation to Mrs Hewlett.

'I have purchased a small safe on your behalf and it will be delivered on Wednesday. The company could not deliver any sooner. Anyway, I'm sure a few days won't matter.'

'It certainly will not.'

They all went into the dining room and took their seats at the circular mahogany table, Mrs Hewlett placing Patrick O'Brien on Mairin's left and James on her right with Marcus seated opposite with an unhappy look on his handsome face.

Marcus directed his conversation to the rest of the party, ignoring her, which was not surprising after receiving her last letter. She looked at his fine strong hands. They had once embraced her. She looked at his mouth. Those lips had once touched hers with fiery passion. Now she could only feel an empty ache in her heart.

Marcus was talking to Mr Hewlett discussing some aspect of the banking world. Mairin sat there watching them. He would marry his Georgiana she thought sadly, and one day he would just be an unhappy memory for her.

She must leave her present employer and find work elsewhere. Constantly meeting Marcus was going to bring her nothing but unhappiness. But how could she do that when Mrs Hewlett depended on her so much? It would be cruel to leave her.

Mairin was in a dilemma.

'And which part of Ireland did your family come from?' Patrick O'Brien was asking her.

'County Monaghan,' she told him. 'A small town called Carrickmacross.'

Patrick O'Brien gave her a big smile.

'Without knowing anything about you I would have guessed you were

Irish or of Irish descent.'

'Why do you say that?' she asked innocently.

'Because Irish girls are beautiful.'

'You are a flatterer Mr O'Brien.'

Marcus was now giving Patrick O'Brien a very hostile look. Mairin had to look away. It was with relief that Mr Hewlett started talking about the problems of the Maoris.

'Let's face it, they were cheated out of their land.' Mr Hewlett looked round the table.

'I beg to differ,' announced Patrick O'Brien. 'Everything was legal and above board.'

The argument went on and on. When Mairin looked across at Marcus the unhappy look was still there.

The clock at the end of the room struck half past ten, and Mairin felt nothing but relief when Mrs Hewlett rose to her feet and announced she had enjoyed the evening and would be retiring for the night. She gave Mairin a nod which meant she was to accompany her. Mairin stood up and bid everyone good night.

Then Patrick O'Brien announced he too would be leaving. He had to return to Christchurch.

The three of them left the room, Mairin could barely look at Marcus. They walked into the entrance hall. Gilbert opened the front door for Patrick O'Brien. Outside she could see his carriage and driver waiting.

Mrs Hewlett and Mairin started to climb the stairs.

'It was a very good evening.' Mrs Hewlett commented turning and smiling at her. 'And I think you made a good impression on Mr O'Brien.'

Mairin remained silent. Mr Patrick O'Brien meant nothing to her. She had no wish to make a good impression on anyone, except of course on Marcus, and that was a waste of time.

'Mr O'Brien is returning to Christchurch tonight,' continued Mrs Hewlett. 'But Mr Howarth will be staying the night and returning to his sheep station tomorrow morning.

'I think now a business meeting will start between my husband, your brother-in-law, and Mr Howarth. I hope your sister does not mind.'

'I think she is used to that sort of thing,' Mairin remarked.

'It's a hard life running a bank.'

Mairin helped Mrs Hewlett to undress. It was a lengthy procedure. Finally she helped the lady into her voluminous nightgown and into bed.

'Good night Mairin,' Mrs Hewlett called in a sleepy voice. 'I have given Ena instructions to bring my breakfast tray at nine thirty tomorrow morning. You have your breakfast in the dining room with my husband and Mr Howarth. I feel like being lazy for once in my life.'

'Good night Mrs Hewlett.'

Mairin left the room closing the door behind her. Downstairs she could hear the sound of men's voices raised in some business discussion. She felt sorry for Oonagh but it was one of her duties to take Mrs Hewlett to bed, and it was now so late she felt sure James would be leaving very soon.

Mairin went to her room and fell asleep, dreaming an unhappy dream about Marcus. When she awoke next morning she was in a thoughtful mood. Am I going to be unhappy like this for the rest of my life she wondered as she went down to the dining room. Marcus was already at the table. His greeting was stiff. He looked tired.

Mairin took her seat opposite him, Marcus giving her a hard look. She could feel a tension gathering in her stomach.

'That letter you . . . ' he began.

Marcus was interrupted by the arrival of Mr Hewlett who looked well rested and a bright smile on his face.

'Good morning Marcus. Good morning Miss Houlihan. I thought last night was a very pleasant evening.'

Suddenly the door was flung open. Ena rushed in, her face white and strained.

'Come quick,' she panted. 'It's the mistress.'

Mr Hewlett, Marcus and Mairin rose swiftly to their feet, followed the maid out of the room and up the stairs.

Mrs Hewlett was lying in her bed, a calm expression on her face. Her eyes were closed, and one of her scarves had been tied around her neck.

She had been strangled! She was dead!

Mairin felt she was going to faint. Her dear employer dead. Suddenly she thought of the jewellery. Going to the bedside cupboard she opened the door.

The cupboard was empty!

5

Mairin turned to find Marcus standing next to her.

'Her jewellery has gone,' Mairin whispered to him. 'The cupboard is empty.'

Marcus took a quick look at the empty cupboard.

'Mr Hewlett, I'm afraid your wife's jewellery is missing,' Marcus informed him. 'We had better get the police and quickly. I'll go myself. It's not far to the central police station in Christchurch.'

Marcus hurried from the room. Mr Hewlett was now kneeling by his wife's bedside holding her hand. Mairin looked across at the dear dead face.

Mrs Hewlett had said she had been like a daughter to her, and in turn Mrs Hewlett had been like a mother to her. Suddenly Mairin felt sick and faint. Mr Hewlett was now prostrate with grief, his hands together praying.

Sensing he wanted to be alone Mairin left the room, and went downstairs and along the back corridor then out to the kitchen hut.

Ena was sat on a stool crying. Aroha was also crying. Mrs Quigley was standing by the window looking grim.

'How could it have happened?' she kept repeating. 'We sleep on the second floor, same corridor as you Miss Houlihan, and we never heard a sound. Did you?'

'No,' Mairin replied, shaking her head. 'Not a sound.'

She felt if she could cry she would feel better. At the moment she was in a state of shock. She had the most excruciating headache, her legs were shaking.

'Here, sit down Miss Houlihan,' said Mrs Quigley. 'There's some hot tea in the pot. I'll pour you a cup.'

The hot tea did make Mairin feel a little better. It must have been about half an hour later they suddenly heard the sound of wheels crunching on the drive.

'That should be Mr Howarth back with the police,' Mairin told them as she left the kitchen hut.

It was Marcus with the police. Mairin met them in the entrance hall and was introduced to Chief Inspector MacGregor and Sergeant MacAllister. With them was a doctor.

Mairin led the men up the stairs to Mrs Hewlett's bedroom. Mr Hewlett was still kneeling by her bedside. His face was grey. The doctor examined Mrs Hewlett and confirmed to the police she had been strangled.

'As death is due to unnatural causes there will have to be an Inquest,' Chief Inspector MacGregor informed them.

He brought out his notebook.

'I will have to ask you a few questions Miss Houlihan. I know it will be distressing for you, but I have to do my duty.'

Mairin gave him a weak smile.

Then glancing across at the grieving

Mr Hewlett, the police officer put the notebook away and stood up.

'I think it will be better for all concerned if we adjourn to another room. In the meantime the doctor will arrange for an undertaker to call.'

Marcus touched Mairin's hand.

'Would you like me to come with you?'

'Yes, I would, if you don't mind.'

They left the room with the two police officers and went downstairs to the drawing room. The questioning began.

'Now Miss Houlihan, tell me all you know.'

'Mrs Hewlett's jewellery is missing.'

The Chief Inspector gave her a sharp look.

'Where was it kept?'

'In her bedside cupboard. She had ordered a safe which will be delivered in a few days time.'

'Any valuable pieces?'

'Yes, many. It would be worth a fortune. She was very careless about its

93

safety. She said she trusted everyone.'

The Chief Inspector made his notes. 'Continue Miss Houlihan.'

'Last night Mr and Mrs Hewlett gave a dinner party. Mr Patrick O'Brien and Mr Howarth were invited. Also my sister Oonagh and her husband James Callcott, and of course myself.

'The meal passed without incident. I think the idea of having dinner parties was Mr Hewlett's. He wanted his wife to meet more people. She led a very quiet life.'

'What time did Mrs Hewlett go to bed?' asked Chief Inspector Mac-Gregor.

Mairin paused a moment.

'About ten thirty,' she replied.

'And what exactly are your duties?' the Chief Inspector continued, giving Mairin a curious stare.

She had to tell the truth even though it would embarrass Mr Hewlett.

'I am a teacher, and I was teaching Mrs Hewlett to read and write. By the way, this matter is confidential. Mr

94

Hewlett likes it to be known that I was his wife's companion.'

The Chief Inspector nodded.

'Continue.'

'Last night I accompanied her back to her room and helped her to undress.'

'What did you do then?' the Chief Inspector asked as he busily wrote his notes.

'I went to my room and went to bed.'

'You did not return to the dining room?'

'No,' Mairin replied. 'I did not.'

'So you were the last person to see Mrs Hewlett alive?'

'Yes,' Mairin replied, wondering at the tone of the police officer's voice. There was a sharp edge to it.

'I am deeply upset . . . ' Mairin began.

The Chief Inspector raised his hand.

'We quite understand Miss Houlihan. During the night did you hear anything?'

Mairin shook her head.

'No, not a sound.'

'Who made the discovery?'

'Ena the maid, when she took the breakfast tray to Mrs Hewlett's room.'

'Thank you Miss Houlihan. That is all for the time being. Now Mr Howarth, may I ask you a few questions?'

Mairin left Marcus being questioned by the Chief Inspector and as she walked along the corridor in the direction of the front verandah she suddenly remembered the Maori odd job man bringing logs to Mrs Hewlett's bedroom on Thursday afternoon. No normal person would light a fire in Mrs Hewlett's bedroom during this hot summer.

Had the Maori odd job man discovered the jewellery, murdered Mrs Hewlett, then stolen it? Or was he totally innocent?

Mairin returned to the drawing room, and stood hesitantly outside the door, when suddenly the door opened and Marcus appeared. Behind him were the Chief Inspector and the Sergeant.

They all looked surprised to see Mairin.

'I've just remembered that on Thursday afternoon something curious happened,' Mairin informed them.

The Chief Inspector looked interested.

'And what was that?'

She then proceeded to tell him what had happened.

'I'd better speak to this Maori man. Will you tell him I want to see him.'

Mairin went immediately to the kitchen hut and informed Mrs Quigley that the police wanted to see the man.

Mrs Quigley looked alarmed.

'What's he done?'

'Nothing as yet. The police want to question him about taking logs to Mrs Hewlett's bedroom when the temperature was in the eighties.'

'Ena, go and fetch him. He should be in the vegetable garden.'

Then turning to Mairin she added, 'He's just a simple man. He didn't do it. Anything missing?'

'Her jewellery.'

'Well I never,' she exclaimed. 'So she was murdered for her jewellery.'

Mairin returned to the house and went along the corridor to the front verandah. It was well shaded by tall matai trees. She sat down in one of the basketwork armchairs. She felt exhausted.

Who had murdered Mrs Hewlett? Some desperate person. The jewellery was probably on its way to America or Australia by now. Hearing footsteps on the wooden floor Mairin turned to see Marcus approaching. He sat down in the chair opposite her. He had a strained look on his face.

'The Maori man is now being questioned,' he told Mairin in a quiet voice. 'But I doubt if they will get anything out of him. He doesn't appear to understand much English.' Marcus gave a sigh. 'A day to remember. Well, if you need a lawyer you already have one. From the way Patrick O'Brien looked at you last night you'll probably get his services free.'

Marcus' tone was contemptuous.

Now Mairin felt annoyed.

'Marcus, please understand Patrick O'Brien means nothing to me.'

'They all say that.'

'But I mean it. Mrs Hewlett, God bless her, was trying to do a bit of match making. But it wasn't going to work. I do not feel that way about the man.'

Mairin's tone was sharp, and her cheeks flushed.

Marcus leaned forward and took her hand in his and held it tight.

'Don't get upset. It's just that I get jealous of any man who looks at you. Mairin, don't encourage Patrick O'Brien. Christchurch is a small community and even though I am out on the plains I do hear what is going on. I have heard this man is a lonely widower and looking for a wife.'

'There is no chance I will encourage him.'

'Promise.'

'I promise.'

'I ignored that letter you sent. I miss you. Come back to me.'

'That is exactly what I want to do. But there is one large obstacle in the way. Marcus you are engaged to someone else. You can offer me nothing, except a secret furtive love affair. I don't want that.'

'Things are going to change. Believe me. Now I must be going. I have to get back. There could be problems that only I can deal with. I'll write to you.'

'Write to my sister's address. There is now no reason for me to continue living in this house.'

Marcus made a quick note of Oonagh's address, then giving her a kiss on the lips, he was gone, striding across the yard to the stables where his black stallion awaited him.

With a heavy heart Mairin watched him ride out of the yard and down the drive, then turning, she left the verandah and walked across to the main entrance hall. Here she found the doctor.

'Miss Houlihan, the undertakers will be here during the next couple of hours. They will make the funeral arrangements. Good day to you.'

Just then Sergeant MacAllister appeared.

'Miss Houlihan, we are having great difficulty in understanding the Maori man. We may have to get an interpreter. Have you noticed any sign of a break in?'

'No I haven't, but I think you ought to see Mrs Quigley the housekeeper.'

The Chief Inspector joined them as they walked down the corridor then out to the kitchen hut. On opening the door Mrs Quigley was making pastry and Ena was at the sink washing up.

Mrs Quigley looked up alarmed at the sight of the two police officers.

'Mrs Quigley, have you seen any signs of a break in?' the Chief Inspector asked her.

Mrs Quigley shook her head.

'No I haven't.' Then she paused. 'Just a moment, when I came down this morning, we sleep on the second floor, the back door was unlocked. I always lock it last thing at night. At least I told Ena to do it.' Turning to Ena she added: 'Ena, did you lock the back door last night?'

'Yes Mrs Quigley.'

'Are you telling the truth?' Her voice was suspicious.

'I am telling the truth,' protested Ena. 'I did lock the back door last night.'

'Where does the Maori man sleep?' asked the Chief Inspector.

'In this kitchen hut,' replied Mrs Quigley. 'Do you think he did it?'

The Chief Inspector did not reply.

Mairin left the kitchen hut with the two police officers and they reentered the house returning to the drawing room.

'Is there anything else you can tell me Miss Houlihan?' asked the Chief Inspector. 'Anything. You may regard it as unimportant but it could be vital evidence.'

Mairin thought hard.

'On Saturday afternoon a second hand furniture man called. Mrs Hewlett wanted to get rid of a few items of furniture.'

'Which company was it?' asked the Chief Inspector.

'Hancock of Limerick Street.'

The Chief Inspector made notes then nodded: 'Continue.'

'The man arrived and took a few pieces of furniture away.'

'Were you present when this happened?'

'Part of the time. Mrs Hewlett did leave the man alone in her bedroom for a few minutes whilst she talked to me in her sitting room.'

The Chief Inspector looked thoughtful.

'I'll just have a word with Mr Hewlett, then we'll be leaving.'

The two police officers left the drawing room and walked away down the corridor in the direction of Mr Hewlett's study.

The day was a nightmare.

A short while later Mairin was sitting in Mrs Hewlett's sitting room when she heard the police vehicles being driven away. She was just wondering what her next move should be. It was now obvious that her services were no longer required when Ena came into the room and told her that Mr Hewlett wished to see her.

Mairin went immediately to his study expecting to be informed that she was dismissed when to her surprise Mr Hewlett still looking strained and ill gave her a weak smile and asked her to sit down.

'Now Miss Houlihan, I have been wondering if you would consider working for me for a few months.'

'I'd be pleased to work for you Mr Hewlett.'

'Good. As you know I own the South Island Loan and Savings Bank, and I have a secretary at the bank who deals with my business correspondence. I need someone here to write personal letters for me, and anything connected with the household. Could you deal with that?'

'Yes Mr Hewlett.'

Mr Hewlett looked pleased.

'You commence your duties tomorrow.'

The elderly man sat back for a moment in his chair and heaved a great sigh.

'Today has been a terrible day. I owed everything to Josephine. She did nothing but help and encourage me in the early days. The Inquest will be next week and the undertaker tells me the funeral will be very soon after that. They will let me know the exact date.

'By the way I've been talking to the Chief Inspector and it does appear that you were the last person to see my wife alive. I do advise you get a good lawyer, and I strongly recommend Mr Patrick O'Brien.'

Mairin looked across the desk at Mr Hewlett feeling a little perplexed.

'Why Mr Patrick O'Brien?'

Mr Hewlett regarded Mairin with surprise.

'Because he is the best lawyer in Christchurch, and you certainly need the best. You are in an unenviable position, and you must get a good man to defend you.'

It was no use arguing. Mairin could see his point of view, but Marcus was not going to be pleased. In fact he was going to be furious.

Strange how the death of Mrs Hewlett had changed their relationship and brought them closer together.

'I have taken the liberty of writing to Mr O'Brien,' Mr Hewlett continued. 'Arranging for you to see him at his Christchurch office tomorrow morning at ten o'clock. Gilbert will take you. I will pay the fees.'

She did not sleep well that night. It had never occurred to her that she would require a lawyer. How could she possibly wish to harm a dear lady of whom she had become very fond?

The following morning Mairin only

had to wait a few minutes before the clerk showed her into Patrick O'Brien's office. She felt a little nervous but Patrick O'Brien standing behind his desk with his hand outstretched, a welcoming smile on his face soon put Mairin at her ease.

'Sit down Miss Houlihan,' he said indicating a chair before his desk.

It was a warm sunny morning with the sunshine streaming in through the window. It was hard to believe that only two days ago Mrs Hewlett had been alive and well.

'Mr Hewlett will have informed you that he has appointed me to be your lawyer,' Patrick O'Brien told her, a warm friendly smile still on his face. 'At the Inquest the Coroner will be asking you questions and I will advise you how to reply. First your full name.'

'Mairin Saoirse Houlihan.'

'Your occupation.'

'I'm a teacher.'

'On the night in question I remember you leaving the dining room with Mrs

Hewlett. I presume to help her prepare for bed.'

Mairin nodded.

'After you left her, did you retire to bed yourself?'

'Yes I did.'

'And where is your room?'

'On the second floor, next to Mrs Quigley.'

'And you heard nothing?'

'Not a sound.'

'Where did the Maori man sleep?'

'The Maori man slept in the kitchen.'

'How long had you known where Mrs Hewlett kept her jewellery?'

'It was only Wednesday of last week. James Callcott, my brother-in-law, he works for Mr Hewlett, he called to discuss Mrs Hewlett making her will. He asked to see where she kept her jewellery and she showed him her bedside cupboard. Up to that time I had no idea where she kept her jewellery. James of course reprimanded her and told her she must keep her jewellery in a safe. She finally agreed to let him buy one on her behalf. It will be delivered this week.'

She gave Patrick O'Brien a sad smile.

'A week too late unfortunately. Thank you Miss Houlihan. Rest assured I will do my utmost to help you. Oh by the way, did she leave you anything in her will?'

'She told me that she would leave me her butterfly brooch.'

Patrick O'Brien then stood up and shook her hand. Mairin felt he held her hand too tightly and too long.

She left the building wondering if she should have mentioned her brother-in-law. She was now implicating him and Oonagh. If the police knew they had serious financial problems it would be a grave situation indeed for them. And also they were planning to emigrate to Australia.

Suddenly Mairin felt a chill around her heart. She did not want to think ill of James. As far as she knew he was an honest hard working man.

When they arrived at Worcester

House Mrs Quigley gave Mairin instructions to go immediately to Mr Hewlett's study. She found him at his desk, a grave expression on his face.

'How did you get on with O'Brien?' he asked in a sharp voice.

She then proceeded to tell him everything she had told Patrick O'Brien.

'Now I have to go to my Christchurch office and shall be away for several days. I have so much work to do I shall be working late in the evenings and staying at the Colonial Inn. Bad news travels fast and the first letters of condolence have arrived.

'Will you answer them? You will find writing paper and envelopes, pens and ink in Mrs Hewlett's sitting room.'

Mr Hewlett then handed Mairin a notebook and pencil and gave instructions on how to answer a number of other letters private and not connected with the bank. He seemed to be very popular in Christchurch society.

Mairin went to Mrs Hewlett's sitting

room and commenced the letter writing. Suddenly the door opened and James entered the room. He had a weary expression on his face.

'Mairin, I have been interviewed by the police about the old lady. I can't understand it. They have told me I ought to get a lawyer because I will be called to the stand at the Inquest.'

'James, I had to tell them you asked Mrs Hewlett where she kept her jewellery. I had to tell the police everything.'

'Of course you did. I'm not blaming you.' James gave a sigh. 'You and I were the only people who knew where she kept her jewellery. Haven't I got enough worries without this?'

The following day after Mairin had completed her letter writing, she went and stood at the window looking out onto the lawn and the little stream that ran through the front garden. It was so obvious that James and herself were not the only people who knew where Mrs Hewlett had kept her jewellery. So who had killed her and stolen her jewellery?

She thought of the staff. There was Gilbert, Ena, Mrs Quigley, Aroha, the Maori odd job man. It could be anyone of them. They all had access to Mrs Hewlett's rooms.

On Saturday afternoon Gilbert took Mairin to Oonagh's house for the weekend. On arrival she found Oonagh distraught with worry.

'Have you heard the latest?' she asked Mairin as they walked into the sitting room.

'Are you going to tell me bad news?' Mairin asked in a depressed voice as she sat down next to her worried looking sister. 'I think you are going to tell me James will have to attend the Inquest and get himself a lawyer.'

Oonagh nodded.

'James couldn't possibly have murdered Mrs Hewlett. You agree with me?'

'Of course I do. James is the kindest, gentlest man you could ever know.'

Mairin put her arm around her sister.

'Everything is going to be all right. I know it is.'

Mairin didn't believe a word she was saying. She had to try to cheer her up, look on the bright side, but James certainly needed a good lawyer.

6

When James came home later that evening he informed Mairin he had consulted a lawyer to act for him.

'I wish I had never mentioned the bloody jewellery,' he exclaimed in an angry voice. 'I wouldn't be in this mess now.' He placed his hand wearily on his forehead.

'I ask myself for the hundredth time, who did it? What do you think Mairin?'

'I am suspicious of the Maori man and Mr Hancock, the second hand furniture man,' Mairin replied fervently. 'To my knowledge Mr Hewlett had little interest in the furniture in his wife's bedroom. Mr Hancock told me Mr Hewlett wrote to him several months ago.'

'When you are on the stand Mairin, tell them everything. Every little detail.'

The following morning before Mairin

went to church she wrote a beseeching letter to Marcus trying to explain the difficult situation she was in.

On Monday morning she left for a final appointment with Patrick O'Brien.

'Now Miss Houlihan, you have nothing to worry about. Get there in good time. Are you staying the night at your brother-in-law's house?'

He gave Mairin a steady, reassuring look.

'Yes I am.'

'Good. Now just answer the questions the coroner will put to you in a clear, unhesitating voice. Just tell the truth and you will have nothing to fear. Now relax.'

The following morning Mairin arrived early at the Court House. The policeman on the door showed her into a crowded waiting room. It was already hot.

At ten o'clock precisely the coroner entered the court room and proceedings began. Mairin sat there, in the small waiting room, a policeman at the door, her head aching. At last her name was called, the policeman escorting her into the courtroom and she took the stand.

'You are Mairin Saoirse Houlihan?' enquired the coroner, an elderly man with a stern expression.

Nearby she could see two rows of men in dark suits. They must be the jury.

'I am,' she replied in a quiet voice.

'Speak up. I can't hear you.'

'I am Mairin Saoirse Houlihan,' Mairin repeated in a louder voice.

'What was your occupation in Mr Hewlett's household?'

'I was Mrs Hewlett's companion.'

'Were you on good terms with Mrs Hewlett?'

'I had a good relationship with Mrs Hewlett.'

'Was she leaving you anything in her will?'

'Yes. A butterfly brooch.'

'Did this upset you?'

'Certainly not.'

'Can you tell me of anything you regarded as suspicious just prior to Mrs Hewlett's death?'

Mairin followed Patrick O'Brien's instructions and told him everything she knew. She spoke of the strange behaviour of the Maori odd job man. The coroner listened.

'Anything else?'

She then told him about the second hand furniture man. There was a long pause whilst the coroner made his notes, then he looked up at Mairin.

'When did you first learn where Mrs Hewlett kept her jewellery?'

'When Mr Callcott called to discuss with Mrs Hewlett the making of her will.'

'When was that?'

'The Wednesday before Mrs Hewlett's death.'

'How did the matter arise?'

'James, that is, Mr Callcott, asked where she kept her jewellery. He was concerned about its safety.'

'And Mrs Hewlett showed you where

she kept her jewellery?'

'That is correct.'

'Did you tell anyone?'

'I told no one.'

There was a pause whilst the coroner looked at his notes.

'It has come to my notice that you Miss Houlihan have recently arrived in New Zealand under the government scheme of the recently formed employment agency for women.

'You are a penniless immigrant, your position in the Hewlett family as Mrs Hewlett's companion was temporary. And we have learnt that your only relations in this country, your sister and her husband, are leaving for Australia.'

The coroner paused, then looked up from his notes.

'That is all. You may go.'

Mairin left the stand feeling distinctly worried. She could see the newspaper reporters scribbling their notes ready for tomorrow's edition. What the coroner had just told the court would be read by everyone in Christchurch tomorrow morning. But more than that the coroner had definitely made it look as though she and James were implicated.

James was due to take the stand and answer the same sort of questions in the afternoon.

The courtroom was now feeling extremely hot and stuffy. Mairin felt desperate for fresh air, her head was throbbing. She asked a policeman on the door if she would be required again. He made enquiries and came back with the reply she would not be required again that day but would be required tomorrow.

Mairin walked back to Oonagh's house. The fresh air and exercise made her feel a little better, and her headache started to clear. How much longer would this torment continue?

James returned in the early evening and had little to say. He looked depressed.

The following morning Mairin and James were back in the courtroom whilst Mr Hancock and the Maori odd job man were interrogated. The Maori man had to have an interpreter. This caused a certain amount of delay.

The jury finally left to consider their verdict. Five hours elapsed and there was still no news. It was now early evening, when suddenly an inner door was flung open and the jury returned entering the courtroom in single file, taking their seats.

The chief juryman stood up and announced their verdict.

'It has been unanimously agreed that Mrs Hewlett was murdered. Her companion Miss Mairin Houlihan is to be held on remand on suspicion of murdering her. Bail of three hundred dollars is available. If this is forthcoming, the suspect will be obliged to report weekly to the Christchurch police.

'The case will be heard at the Assizes in Christchurch before a judge and jury as soon as possible.'

She was to be held on remand on

suspicion of murdering her dear departed Mrs Hewlett who had shown her nothing but kindness!

Had the jury gone mad?

Her legs were shaking so badly she had to sit down. Suddenly she saw Marcus talking to Mr Hewlett in an imploring manner.

A minute later Mr Hewlett and Marcus walked across to the clerk of the court and spoke to him. Patrick O'Brien joined them. Then the clerk stood up and spoke to the coroner. The coroner banged his hammer and the buzz of conversation in the court room ceased.

'I have just been informed that Mr Howarth has agreed to stand bail for Miss Houlihan.'

Patrick O'Brien made his way through the crowd to her.

'Miss Houlihan, the conditions will be that you will have to live at Worcester House, leaving the house only with Mr Hewlett's permission, and never travelling further than the environs of Christchurch.'

Patrick O'Brien escorted Mairin from the court house to Mr Hewlett's waiting phaeton. She climbed aboard and a few moments later Mr Hewlett appeared, seated himself next to her and they set off.

'It has been a sad day for you Miss Houlihan, but rest assured I will do everything I can to help you. I am certain there has been a dreadful mistake. It was so obvious that a burglar stole my dear wife's jewellery then murdered her.'

The day was unreal, her heart was beating too fast. Mr Hewlett turned a grave face towards her.

'Christchurch has only one small gaol and it is overcrowded. The judiciary of this area decided the answer to the problem was suitable prisoners to be held on remand. Now I don't want Mr Howarth to lose his money.'

'I will do everything I can to cooperate, and I cannot thank you enough for your kindness.'

When they arrived at Worcester House Mairin and Mr Hewlett went straight to his study where he handed her a pile of letters of condolence.

'Answer these letters and remember the funeral is on Monday. And perhaps you could help Mrs Quigley.'

'Certainly Mr Hewlett.'

'And regarding the forthcoming trial, believe me, you couldn't have a better lawyer than Patrick O'Brien. I am now going back to the bank, and will return on Sunday. Good day to you Miss Houlihan.'

For the rest of the week Mairin spent her time writing letters on behalf of Mr Hewlett to the many kind people of Christchurch who had expressed their sorrow at the death of Mrs Hewlett.

The fact that Marcus had paid the bail money took away some of the anguish. To do such a thing she thought as she went about her daily duties he must really love her.

On Saturday morning after breakfast

Mairin went straight to the kitchen hut to see if she could help. As the funeral was in two days time, she felt Mrs Quigley would be requiring assistance.

Many mourners were expected. Geese had been killed and were being plucked and made ready for the oven.

'Could I help?' asked Mairin as she sat down next to Ena.

'You certainly can. More hands make light work. We're going to cook the geese in a slow oven. It will take the best part of the day. Meantime plenty of dish washing.'

A younger version of Mrs Quigley entered the kitchen.

'This is my sister Nellie,' Mrs Quigley announced. 'She's come to help.'

Nellie looked across at Mairin.

'I read in the paper about you Miss Houlihan,' she began shyly. 'I think it's disgraceful. I know from my sister you are a very nice, kind woman and wouldn't harm a fly.'

'Thank you Nellie for your kind

words. You need to tell that to the police.'

On the day of the funeral, Mairin was up early, and dressed quickly in her black mourning gown and black bonnet. Gilbert was in a hurry to get to the church afraid that all the stables in Christchurch might be full.

Mairin's headache returned. Keeping herself busy and filling her mind with happy memories of Mrs Hewlett had helped her through the week. Now sadness returned as she stepped from the carriage and entered the crowded church.

All of Christchurch seemed to be there, the city council, the mayor, members of the police force, and many private citizens, for as owner of the South Island Loan and Savings Bank, many people had entrusted their savings with Mr Hewlett, or been grateful for the loan he had given them to buy their property or business.

The news of Mrs Hewlett's murder had shocked Christchurch. Mairin and

Mrs Quigley entered through the main door into the crowded interior, an organ was playing softly. As they took their seats some people cast Mairin angry looks, others gave her a sullen stare.

The coffin bearers entered the church. Hymns were sung, prayers read. Mr Hewlett sat in front of Mairin and Mrs Quigley.

After the service Mr Hewlett stood at the graveside, his eyes full of sorrow. The coffin was lowered into the grave, then the priest's solemn voice uttered the following words:

'Ashes to ashes, dust to dust . . . '

Mairin's eyes filled with tears. Many of the wreaths were white puawhananga, one of Mrs Hewlett's favourite flowers, then Gilbert gave the signal to leave for they had to be at Worcester House before the mourners arrived.

When Mairin entered Worcester House she found that Mrs Quigley had already prepared the refreshments for the mourners. Now all she wanted was to be alone.

Suddenly she saw Marcus enter the room, looking very handsome in his dark mourning suit. The moment he saw her he walked across to her. She gave him an embarrassed look.

'Thank you for standing bail for me. I just don't know how to thank you.'

'I do,' he replied giving her a mischievous smile.

'I'm not in the mood for jokes, not today.'

'Sorry, I didn't intend to offend you. You are looking very attractive in your dark mourning gown,' he added in a low voice. Then his face took on a more serious look.

'What a stupendous mistake the jury made. Now you really need a good lawyer.'

At that moment one of the city aldermen approached.

'May I speak to you Mr Howarth?'

'Excuse me a moment Mairin.'

In the crowd milling around the room Mairin turned to see Oonagh hurrying towards her, an unhappy expression on her face. She looked as though she had been crying.

'What has upset you Oonagh? Can you tell me what it is?'

Oonagh did not answer, but stood there biting her lip.

'Where is James?' Mairin asked looking around. 'I did not see him in church.'

'Mairin, I must speak to you confidentially. Could we go outside?'

Mairin led the way out into the warm sunshine to stand in the shade of the matai tree.

'What is it Oonagh? You've been crying. Is Hannah all right?'

Oonagh's eyes filled with tears.

'It's nothing to do with Hannah.'

'Oonagh, what is it? You must tell me.'

'James has gone.'

'Gone where?' asked Mairin feeling perplexed.

'Australia. He went this morning and will be writing. We have been planning for a long time to go there and join his parents, but why the sudden departure? Why couldn't he wait until the trial is over? I'm positive he will be required to give evidence and he won't be here.'

Mairin thought for a moment, puzzled at this latest development.

'Is it anything to do with financial problems?'

Oonagh shrugged her shoulders.

'If I ask any questions he won't discuss it with me. I look after the house and the baby and James looks after the money, or he is supposed to,' she added with a frown.

Mairin gave a sigh.

'I'm sorry to hear this, but please don't worry Oonagh I'm sure you will hear from him soon. You know he loves you and Hannah.'

'Sometimes I wonder.'

They walked back into the house. Now Mairin felt suspicious of James. Why suddenly go to Australia? He had a good position in Mr Hewlett's bank, a pleasant house, a loving wife and child.

Of course he had financial problems. But surely going to Australia could have waited until after the trial.

Anyway, he was going to be in trouble with the police. Guests were now leaving. Mairin saw Marcus in the hall.

'I'll say goodbye,' said Oonagh. 'Will I see you on Saturday as usual?'

'I hope so.'

As Oonagh hurried away Marcus walked across to her.

'The funeral went off without a hitch. I wouldn't allow any newspaper reporters in the church.'

'Thank you Marcus.'

'Could we talk somewhere more private than this?' he asked as people pushed past him.

Mairin nodded.

'Follow me.'

She led the way upstairs to Mrs Hewlett's sitting room, closed the door and sank into the armchair by the empty fireplace, beckoning Marcus to take a seat opposite.

'What a relief it is over,' she told him as she untied her bonnet and placed it on the occasional table near her. 'And what a sad day.'

'I really wanted you to live with me on the sheep station,' Marcus replied. 'Just the two of us. But as you have to report to the Christchurch police weekly it was out of the question.

'I have written to Miss Stuart Erskine and told her I do not wish to marry her. The engagement announcement was made by my mother against my wishes. Unfortunately I have since received a letter from her parents stating they are going to sue me.'

Marcus rose to his feet, so did Mairin. There was a lock of dark hair straggled across his forehead. He looked worried. Mairin raised her hand and pushed the lock of hair away and as she did so Marcus grabbed her hand.

'If anything happens to you I'll kill myself,' he whispered.

Then his arms went around her, holding her close to him, his thighs pressed against hers.

'Remember I love you,' he whispered. 'I don't know when I'll be able to see you again. I'll be writing to you.'

Then giving her a warm kiss on the lips, he turned and walked out of the room.

Life returned to normal, as normal as it ever could be for Mairin, a day to day existence, she could never think of the future. But whenever she thought of Marcus she felt a strange shivery tingling down her spine. It was a feeling she had never experienced before.

It was agreed with Mr Hewlett that at weekends Mairin could visit her sister in Christchurch, a thirty minute drive from Worcester House.

It was the first Saturday morning after the funeral. Gilbert took Mairin to Oonagh's house in the trap arranging to pick her up early on Monday morning. After reporting to the Christchurch police, Mairin returned to the house. Oonagh was sat on the edge of her chair looking very tense.

'Chief Inspector MacGregor has just called,' she informed Mairin. 'He wants to see James for further questioning.'

Mairin touched her sister's arm.

'Did you tell him he is in Australia?'

Oonagh nodded.

'He said he had no right to go there. He knew he was going to be called as a witness. He wanted his new address.'

'Did you give it to him?'

'I gave him James' parents' address. That is the only address I have. I had to Mairin. He demanded it. I suppose I've got James into trouble now.'

'You had to tell him Oonagh.'

On Monday morning Gilbert drove Mairin back to Worcester House where further letters of condolence were awaiting her. Mairin attended to them immediately, but all the time she was worried about James.

Why did the police want to see him for further questioning? Because they were suspicious of him?

In the evening she ate supper with Mrs Quigley and Ena in the kitchen hut. Aroha entered the hut, her flax reed skirt swishing as her bare feet pattered across the wooden floor. They all sat down at the well scrubbed table.

Aroha proudly informed them all she would soon be getting married to the Maori odd job man and moving to North Island to be with his family.

'Congratulations,' Mrs Quigley told her. 'We'll be sorry to see you go. We'll miss your stories. Any more?'

Aroha nodded giving them a big smile, and told the story of four mountains, Tongariro, Taranaki, Tauhara and Puutauaki who fought for the love of a female mountain. When Aroha had finished her story telling Mrs Quigley turned to Mairin.

'Miss Houlihan, you ought to write these stories down and make them into a book.'

Mairin spent the rest of the week answering letters, doing the household accounts, and in the evening making herself a gown out of the pink rose bud curtains that Mrs Hewlett had given to her. She felt if she didn't keep herself busy she would go mad.

Life was now like living in a dark tunnel with no light at the end.

Almost a week had past and there had been no letter from Marcus. He had said he would write. He must know how unhappy she felt, waiting for the trial.

When she went to bed at night a terrible sense of loneliness for Marcus and bereavement for Mrs Hewlett overcame her, Mrs Hewlett had been not only an employer but a friend. Every night she prayed fervently for the culprit to be found.

On Saturday morning when Mairin arrived at Oonagh's for the weekend she found a letter awaiting her from Patrick O'Brien inviting her to dinner at the Colonial Inn that evening.

It was only a short walk to the Colonial Inn from Oonagh's house. On arrival Mairin seated herself in a chair by the window in the hotel foyer.

Suddenly she saw a group of six

people enter the inn. There were four men one of whom was Mr Hewlett, and two women. One woman was elderly and plain, whilst the other was young, tall, slim, with a great abundance of auburn hair. She was beautiful.

At that moment Patrick O'Brien appeared, walking quickly across the foyer.

'I'm so sorry to have kept you waiting,' he apologised.

'That is perfectly all right. Mr O'Brien, do you see the group entering the restaurant? One of the men is Mr Hewlett and there are two women. One is very beautiful with auburn hair. Who is she?'

Patrick O'Brien smiled.

'That is Miss Georgiana Stuart Erskine. It's the monthly meeting of the Christchurch Charity Committee. They have pledged themselves to help the poor of Christchurch. Mr Hewlett has been a member for many years.'

The beautiful Georgiana made Mairin feel plain and dowdy. Men would fall in love with her with ease she thought as she watched the group take their seats in the restaurant. Was Marcus telling the truth that he had no wish to marry her?

It was a pleasant meal and after they had eaten Patrick O'Brien made various suggestions as to how he was going to conduct her defence. Then finally he gave her a warm smile.

'May I call you Mairin, and will you call me Patrick?'

'If you wish,' Mairin replied, feeling a little uncomfortable. The situation was starting to get out of control.

They left the hotel. Patrick called a cab and took her back to Oonagh's. In the cab Patrick gazed softly at her.

'I'm a lonely man,' he whispered. 'I want to be more than a lawyer to you.'

The cab stopped outside Oonagh's house. Patrick turned his kind, gentle face to her.

'The moment I know the date of the trial I will write to you. And think about what I said.'

Mairin stepped out of the cab. 'Good night Patrick.' Mairin entered the house and went up to her room. She needed Patrick as a lawyer, not a lover. And as for Marcus when she thought of him now, she experienced a feeling of sadness. He had told her he loved her, but there would never be a proposal of marriage.

Nothing had changed.

She undressed and went to bed, and the moment her head touched the pillow the tears came. She cried for a long time until exhaustion overcame her and she slept.

The following morning Mairin attended the Sunday service with Oonagh.

'I'm so worried that the police want to interview James,' Oonagh told Mairin as they came out of the church. 'They'll probably contact the Australian police. James had to ask Mrs Hewlett where she kept her jewellery. He was concerned about its safety.'

'Of course he was. It's probably just routine questioning, and nothing to worry about.'

'How was your dinner engagement with Patrick O'Brien last night? You don't look particularly happy today. Can you tell me about it?'

'Oonagh it was a very pleasant evening with Patrick. Yes, he wants me to call him Patrick.' Mairin gave a sigh. 'I saw Miss Georgiana Stuart Erskine arrive with the Christchurch Charity Committee. One of their monthly meetings. I had no idea she was so beautiful. She made me feel quite plain. Oh Oonagh, Marcus has not asked me to marry him and I don't think he ever will.'

'Forget him.'

It was in the early evening. Mairin was awaiting the arrival of Gilbert to take her back to Worcester House when she started thinking about James and the police request for further questioning.

Oonagh came in from the garden

with Hannah in her arms.

'You are waiting for Gilbert?'

Mairin nodded.

'Oonagh, do you remember the night when you and James came to dinner at Worcester House, the night poor Mrs Hewlett was murdered?'

Oonagh sat down next to her on the window seat.

'Mairin, I'll never forget it! But why do you ask?'

'I was just thinking of the incidents of that evening. After I left the dining room with Mrs Hewlett about half past ten, did James leave the dining room at any time?'

Oonagh had to pause and think.

'Yes he did. It was about half past eleven. He had to go to Mr Hewlett's study to collect some letters and reports.'

'How long was he away?'

'It must have been half an hour. I did think he was away a long time.'

'Why did it take half an hour to find some letters and reports?'

'I don't know.' Then Oonagh paused a moment. 'I've just remembered. He said he had had a lot of trouble finding the letters and reports. He returned carrying them in a leather case.'

7

A frightening thought suddenly entered Mairin's head. Did James do it? Murder poor Mrs Hewlett and steal her jewellery? Oonagh had told her they were desperately short of money just before Mrs Hewlett's death, and now he had suddenly gone to Australia.

'Something the matter Mairin?' Oonagh asked as she picked up some of Hannah's dolls that had been left in an armchair. 'You are looking very concerned.'

They went outside and took a walk around the front garden.

'Why did James suddenly go to Australia?'

'His parents have been asking him to join them ever since they went. They are managing an accommodation house. I'm waiting for him to write telling me when Hannah and I can join him.'

Gilbert arrived. Mairin bid Oonagh and Hannah goodbye and started the journey back to Worcester House. Gilbert gave her a friendly smile.

'I hear that the Christchurch Charity Committee are going to arrange a grand ball in Christchurch. It will be very soon to raise money for the poor.'

Mairin gave him a weak smile. She felt some comment was expected of her.

'I didn't realise what a lot of rich people there are in Christchurch.

'Descendants of the first settlers,' Gilbert told her. 'They got good land cheap and poor land free.'

Mairin went to bed that night in a puzzled frame of mind. Mr Hewlett had asked her to stay on to reply to the letters of condolence, now all those replies had been written.

At the Inquest he had agreed to allow her to live at Worcester House under his supervision. As she had to continue living here until the trial, how was she going to pass the time?

The following morning Mairin went downstairs. It was late and no breakfast tray had been brought up to her sitting room. In the entrance hall she found a letter addressed to her. It was from Marcus. Hastily she torn open the envelope and read the following.

' . . . I now feel I do not care if the Stuart Erskines try to ruin me. Let them go ahead. You are all I want . . . '

Mairin felt so happy as she went down the corridor, crossed the back lawn and entered the kitchen hut. Mrs Quigley gave Mairin a weary look.

'The master is having another dinner party tomorrow night.'

'Could I help you Mrs Quigley? I'll start now.'

'Me too,' added Aroha. 'We all help each other. And as we work I can tell stories. They have never been written,' she added smiling at Mairin. 'We tell our children and they tell their children.

'It has been like that since the beginning of time when the gods first looked down on us.'

What a strange life she led Mairin thought later in the morning as she polished the dining table. Living in this delightful house on the edge of the bush, but held on remand on suspicion of murdering her dear employer. It was like living a peculiar sort of horrible dream.

She then thought of James. On that fateful night when Mrs Hewlett had been murdered it was strange that James had taken such a long time to find the correspondence in Mr Hewlett's study.

Had he disturbed Mrs Hewlett when in the act of stealing her jewellery been forced to murder her and had now gone to Australia to sell the jewellery? James had never given her the impression of being a violent man, and yet, how well do we know people, people who are close to us? They can be pleasant, respectable, and successfully hide the evil side of their nature.

Oonagh would know James better than anyone, but she had never told her of any cause she had for concern, she had always been frank and open with Mairin. Had Oonagh suspicions about James, and was keeping it to herself.

Mr Hewlett arrived at Worcester House the following afternoon. Gilbert came into Mairin's sitting room and informed her she was required in Mr Hewlett's study.

Mr Hewlett was sat behind his desk. He gave her a brief nod and handed her a pile of letters. There was a tense look on his face.

'I thought the kind letters of condolence had ceased. Here are some more. It is never ending. You know how to reply to them. Sign on my behalf.'

And so the days past uneventfully. Helping Mrs Quigley whenever she could, helping Mr Hewlett with his correspondence, sewing in the evenings and all the time the terrible cloud of the forthcoming trial hanging over her.

At the weekend Mairin went as usual to Oonagh's. She still could not get rid of the feeling of suspicion about James.

It was when they were having afternoon tea that Mairin could not help bringing up the subject:

'Oonagh, you told me James said very little about his financial affairs. What a pity he did not take you into his confidence.'

'Yes, James told me very little. Often he had to work in the evenings and did not come home until late. Sometimes it was past midnight. Why do you ask?'

'Why should Mr Hewlett keep him working till past midnight?'

Oonagh shrugged her shoulders.

'I don't know. Mairin, I have been doing a lot of thinking about the night Mrs Hewlett was murdered.' Oonagh gave Mairin a worried look.

'Something else happened?'

'I'm just stating facts. When we left Worcester House that night it was about midnight. Marcus Howarth, I understand, stayed the night.'

'What are you trying to say?'

'He might have done it — murdered Mrs Hewlett.'

'What possible motive could he have had?'

'You don't know this but Mrs Hewlett hated Marcus Howarth. She was strongly opposed to Mr Hewlett making him a director of the bank and wanted the directorship cancelled.'

'But why?'

'He was a snob, brother of Lord Howarth, and next in line for the title and inheritance. Mrs Hewlett came from very humble beginnings.'

'So did we,' protested Mairin.

'I know our father was only a coal miner, but I did hear Mrs Hewlett's mother went out to Australia as a convict. Mrs Hewlett would have been a small child at the time.'

'But why should Marcus be upset if his directorship was cancelled?'

'Because he needs the generous fees Mr Hewlett pays him.'

Mairin felt puzzled.

'But he's a sheep farmer with thousands of acres.'

'He was only able to buy a short land

lease, so I have heard, which is coming up for renewal very soon and a new long lease or freehold could cost a great deal of money.'

'Surely he could afford it.'

'People have less money than you think.'

Mairin's head was starting to ache.

'If you go to the police with this story the situation will look very bad for Marcus.'

'I've already been.'

Mairin gazed at her sister in astonishment. She had always known Oonagh did not like him, now she knew Oonagh hated Marcus. Hannah started to cry on the verandah.

'You shouldn't have done it Oonagh.'

Oonagh looked crestfallen.

'I know. But I have been very worried about James. They are obviously suspicious of him.'

'I'll put Hannah to bed.'

Mairin bathed Hannah, fed her, then took her upstairs to her cot. How could Oonagh, her own sister, have done such a terrible thing?

She returned to the sitting room, her spirits low. Oonagh gave her a sad smile.

'You'll never forgive me, will you?'

The following morning Mairin went to the Sunday service at the nearby church. Hannah had developed a heavy cold and had cried a good deal of the night which meant Oonagh had had very little sleep and begged to be excused. After the service Mairin walked out into the street and suddenly she saw Marcus hurrying towards her. He gave her a warm smile and held her hand. She felt her heart thumping in her breast. She was so happy to see him.

'Sorry I haven't written but there have been a lot of problems. Anyway, I thought I'd see you here Mairin. Otherwise I was coming to your sister's. We have a lot to talk about.'

Mairin gave him a happy smile as he took her arm.

'Shall we walk down to the river?' he

asked turning to her.

'Marcus,' Mairin ventured as they walked along the grassy banks of the Avon. She had to tell him.

'My sister has been to the police and made strange accusations about you.'

'I know,' he replied in a quiet voice. 'Why do you think I am in Christchurch?'

'I can't tell you how sorry I am.'

'The woman must be mad. Anyway the accusation would not stand up in a court of law. Do you believe what she has been saying?'

'Of course not,' Mairin replied firmly. 'I never heard such nonsense in my life.'

Marcus grasped her hand, and as he did so a terrible sadness overcame Mairin. She loved this man but he would never be hers.

They continued walking in silence. Suddenly Marcus turned to her:

'You did not commit that vile murder. We will fight it.

'We are the music makers
And we are the dreamers of dreams
Wandering by lone sea breakers,'

Mairin gave him a happy smile and continued:

'Yet we are the movers and shakers
Of the world forever it seems.'

She felt near to tears. 'I'll remember that when I'm standing in the dock in a few weeks time.'

Marcus gave her a stern look.

'As soon as that.'

They returned to Oonagh's house, Marcus bidding her goodbye at the gate.

'I'm not in the mood for meeting your sister at the moment. You understand how I feel.'

'Of course I do Marcus.'

'I will be seeing you soon.'

Mairin watched him hurry down the street then turning she walked the short path to the house entering through the open door.

Oonagh was waiting for her in the sitting room.

'Was that Marcus Howarth with you at the gate?' she enquired.

'Yes,' answered Mairin.

'I thought you had more sense.'

'Oonagh, I love the man.'

'You are a foolish woman.'

'I know I am.'

The two women regarded each other in silence for a moment.

Mairin sat on the settee, Oonagh joined her.

'Will you ever forgive me Mairin?'

Mairin looked at her sister's beseeching face.

'I forgive you.'

Oonagh flung her arms around her sister.

'You're the best sister anyone could ever have.'

At six o'clock as arranged Gilbert arrived in the trap and Mairin returned to Worcester House. The following morning Mairin entered Mr Hewlett's study to see if he had left any work for her to do.

There was nothing on the desk.

She returned to her sitting room wondering how to spend the day when suddenly she remembered the Maori stories Aroha had been telling her and the fact that they had never been written.

So Mairin started writing them. In the afternoon she decided to have a change of occupation and spent her time weeding Mrs Hewlett's favourite flower beds.

In the evening she returned to the task of writing the Maori stories. It must have been about nine o'clock. It was still light when Mairin realised she had used all the paper she had in the sitting room and needed just one more sheet to complete the story.

It was annoying to leave the work unfinished. Mairin went to Mr Hewlett's study. To her disappointment there were no spare sheets of paper on his desk. Suddenly her attention was distracted by the books on the shelves behind his desk.

She went across and studied the titles. One in particular attracted her attention, The Secret History of George the Third.

Mairin took the large volume off the shelf and as she did so she noticed a safe fitted into the wall behind the books. No one had ever told her that Mr Hewlett had a safe hidden behind the books in his study.

Suddenly the door opened and to her amazement Mr Hewlett was standing there, an angry expression on his face.

'What are you doing in my study at this time of night?'

'I'm so sorry Mr Hewlett, but I came in looking for a few spare sheets of paper. I felt you wouldn't mind. I'm writing the stories Aroha has been telling me. I had used up all the paper I had.'

'You are lying,' Mr Hewlett replied in an angry voice, his face red, his hands shaking.

'I'm not Mr Hewlett,' Mairin protested. 'When I realised you did not have any spare sheets of paper, I became intrigued by one of the titles of your books.'

'You are a liar, and untrustworthy. You are dismissed. I am going to Kaikoura for a week and when I return I do not want to see you here.'

And with that he left the room.

8

She had been dismissed and merely because she had gone to Mr Hewlett's study to see if he had any spare sheets of paper, and then as reading history was one of her pleasures she had been attracted to one of the books.

It was hard to believe this had happened. She should have asked permission to take a volume off the shelf. It was good manners. But for such a mild misdemeanour the punishment was too harsh.

Mairin had always seen Mr Hewlett as a firm but kind man, but never one so cruel and unjust. Mrs Hewlett had always had a pleasant word to say about him, and Mairin had considered herself fortunate to be working for him.

She had to get another situation quickly, but how could she when the terms of the bail were that she remained at Worcester House. He must have forgotten in the heat of the moment.

The light was starting to fade as Mairin walked slowly down the corridor and down the stairs, trying to decide what to do.

Marcus! He would help her!

Now feeling much happier about this unreal situation Mairin decided to go across to the kitchen hut to discuss it with Mrs Quigley. Mrs Quigley was alone at the sink washing up.

'I've just been dismissed.'

Mrs Quigley stared at her in disbelief.

'I don't understand. You have to stay here until the trial. Isn't that right?'

'Yes. Mr Hewlett has gone to Kaikoura for a week and I must not be here when he returns.'

'Whatever did you do to upset him so? I always find you a reasonable person.'

Mairin gave her a sad smile.

'Looking at his books in his study,

without his permission.'

She spoke in a bitter tone. Mrs Quigley listened.

'You can't sack someone just because they were looking at your books.'

'Mrs Quigley, I have been happy here, except of course when poor Mrs Hewlett died. That was very sad, and you know I did not do it. I'm not capable of such a vicious act.'

'I know you're not,' sympathised Mrs Quigley. 'And I'd say that in a court of law. What are you going to do?'

Mairin gave a sigh.

'There is always my sister, but she has enough problems of her own. Then there is my previous employer, Mr Howarth. I had decided to go to him, now I am not sure what to do. His sheep station is a long way from Christchurch, and I will be in trouble with the police if they call and find I am not here.'

'Perhaps you should go to see your lawyer,' suggested Mrs Quigley. 'Isn't he called O'Brien? He could advise you. Of course it is up to you.'

Mairin went back into the house and up to her room to pack her few possessions. It was not a good idea to see Patrick. If she went to his house for help, the situation in their private lives could become very complicated indeed. Apart from that it would anger Marcus.

Marcus was the only person who could help her.

Early the following morning after a hurried breakfast with Mrs Quigley Mairin hurried down the drive clutching her carpet bag to the main road to await the Timaru stagecoach.

She was still in a state of shock, still bewildered by the whole series of events; Mrs Hewlett murdered, herself held on remand on suspicion of murdering her dear employer, and now being dismissed.

The stagecoach was on time and Mairin stepped inside. Her travelling companions were mainly farmers and their wives, pleasant hard working people.

In the late evening they approached the Raraia crossroads, just a humble settlement of two weatherboard houses and the nearest crossroad to Marcus' sheep station.

Mairin left her companions of the last twelve hours. They had helped her to forget her troubles, now alone again as she walked the rough track to the entrance of Marcus' sheep station she began to have doubts that she had done the right thing.

She was breaking the bail agreement by leaving Worcester House. But she had been told to leave.

She was in a dilemma!

As she reached the sprawling wooden house she wondered about her friend Zillah and hoped she had fared better. It was dusk as she stepped onto the verandah and knocked at the door with a feeling of trepidation.

Marcus opened the door with a look of astonishment on his face. Immediately his arms were around her, holding her tight.

'Oh Mairin, how wonderful to see you. But what has happened?'

They entered the house. Nothing had changed. The pleasant cosy atmosphere, the polished wooden floors shrewn with gaily coloured rugs, the beautifully carved wooden furniture made by Maori craftsmen arranged around the rooms.

'Now Mairin, tell me why I have this unexpected pleasure.'

Mairin told him everything that had happened whilst Marcus paced the room, frowning heavily.

'There must be another reason why he has dismissed you. One that has escaped your attention. Anyway, we have a serious problem here. The conditions of the bail are that you remain at Worcester House. You should have remained there. It is possible that when Mr Hewlett returns from Kaikoura he will have forgotten all about his loss of temper and his mind be on other matters.

'I'm afraid you are going to be in

trouble with the police. You say Mr Hewlett will be back from Kaikoura in about a week's time. We have a week to decide what to do.'

Mairin looked across at Marcus who was now standing before the empty fireplace, an unhappy expression on his face.

'I'm sorry for the trouble I am causing you . . . ' Mairin began.

'You are no trouble Mairin. You know that. I am very happy to see you.' Then he paused. 'The other day it was an unpleasant experience being questioned by Chief Inspector Macgregor and Sergeant MacAllister. They wanted to know everything, every single thing that happened on the night of that ill fated dinner party. If you know anything for God's sake tell me.'

'The police want to question my brother-in-law. He's in Australia by the way.'

'James Callcott in Australia? What is he doing there?'

'I don't know.'

'To hold you on remand on suspicion of murder is madness,' Marcus retorted. 'To murder the poor lady in order to steal her jewellery must be someone who was in an extremely desperate state for money. Know anyone like that?'

'I know a number of people who are desperate for money but they would not murder for it. Marcus, I was shocked when my sister told me she had been to the police about you.'

Marcus gave a wry smile.

'I now have to give evidence at the trial. Anyway, your worries are far greater than mine.'

Mairin stood up and went across to Marcus. His arms went around her.

'I love you,' she told him.

Marcus touched her hand, their mouths met, then suddenly he was kissing her with such ferocity she was left breathless.

'What are we going to do?' he whispered, his mouth kissing her neck. 'Leave the country?'

'And be on the run for the rest of our lives?'

She picked up one of the candles.

'I'm going to bed,' she told him in a quiet voice.

They stared at each other in silence for a moment, their minds filled with unspoken thoughts and desires. Then it took Mairin all her will power to leave that room and go down the corridor.

It was a strange feeling to be back. Mairin undressed. In a corner of the wardrobe she found a dark blue gown. It wasn't hers. Perhaps at some time in the last few weeks Marcus had engaged a housekeeper who had recently left. It didn't worry her in the least.

She put on her nightgown, blew out the candle, and got into bed. From the little window in the light of a full moon she could see the snowy summits of the distant Southern Alps. It was a beautiful sight.

Mairin lay there a long time, sleep far away, recalling the reason why she had left Marcus' sheep station, which now seemed such a long time ago. She thought of the night he had kissed her so passionately, she had been convinced that she would end up in his bed, but matters had taken a different turn.

She awoke. Something must have disturbed her. The full moon was now behind a bank of clouds and her room was in darkness. Suddenly she could hear voices. Marcus and a woman. They were speaking in a soft tone in the corridor outside her room.

Mairin sat up in bed, tense, listening.

'You told me to come to you,' she heard the woman say.

'You did the right thing,' Marcus replied.

Then their voices trailed away as they walked down the corridor. Then there was silence.

Mairin's heart was thumping in her breast. There was a pulse beating in her head. The woman's voice was vaguely familiar but she could not recall where she had last heard it.

'You told me to come to you' the

woman had told Marcus. What did it mean? Had Marcus acquired a mistress?

Mairin could not sleep for the rest of the night. What a terrible mistake it had been coming here. She loved Marcus and trusted him. Now all the trust had gone. She had to get out of this house and quickly, and it had to be back to Worcester House, much as she dreaded meeting Mr Hewlett again.

Her heart was heavy as she rose early next morning, washed and dressed, her mind filled with bitter unhappy thoughts. Would she never learn her lesson?

Then slipping on her bonnet and cape Mairin silently stole from the house, hurried down the drive to the main road. She knew that some of the hired workers had dogs, but none of them barked. No one knew she had gone.

At the Raraia crossroads about half a mile away she waited. Soon a waggon came lumbering along. Mairin waved to the driver, an elderly man.

'Are you going to Christchurch?' she called.

His waggon was piled high with timber.

'Sure,' he called. 'If you don't mind an uncomfortable seat.'

Mairin clambered up and sat in the empty seat next to him.

'Going to try your fortune in Christchurch?' he asked.

Mairin nodded with a faint smile.

He talked non-stop for the next few hours about his emigration to New Zealand. Mairin welcomed it. It helped to ease the pain in her heart. The old man went on to tell her about the fighting he had done in the Maori wars, his friends who had been killed.

It was dark when the waggoner dropped her off at the turning for Worcester House, and twenty minutes later she was walking up the short drive to the house. She was still deeply hurt by Marcus' betrayal. What else could she think?

The loud humming of the cicadas was coming from the bush and she could smell the strong scent of the mahoe flowers. It was almost like coming home except it wasn't her home any longer.

Mrs Quigley as usual was in the kitchen hut. She was alone.

'Miss Houlihan. I've been so worried about you. Where have you been?'

She moved across to the fire where a large black kettle sat steaming on the hob and made a pot of tea. Mairin sat down at the table, her eyes filled with tears. Mrs Quigley filled a mug with tea and set it before her.

'Drink that.'

Mairin drank.

'It was a terrible mistake.'

Mrs Quigley gave her a curious stare.

'What do you mean? Where did you go?'

'Mr Howarth. I should never have gone.'

'Well, you'll tell me all about it when

you feel like it.' Then Mrs Quigley looked at Mairin keenly. 'Whatever it was it upset you. Will you be staying the night?'

'I think I have no alternative. I have a sister in Christchurch. I don't want to trouble her. She has enough worries without me.'

'As far as I am concerned you can stay here as long as you want. Mr Hewlett dismissing you! I think he's weak in the head.'

Ena entered the kitchen hung up her cape then tied an apron round her waist.

'I read in the paper Mr Howarth has been questioned by the police. I can't think what that could be about. He always seems such a nice gentleman. Why should they question him?' Ena frowned.

'Why do you ask?' enquired Mairin suddenly curious.

'Well, the night poor Mrs Hewlett got murdered, after dinner she went up to her bedroom. Then sometime later she rang her bell.'

'What time would that be?' Mairin asked.

'I think some time between half past eleven and midnight. She wanted a glass of warm milk, so I went downstairs to get it. She usually likes warm milk at bedtime. Helps her to get to sleep, so she used to tell me. I felt a bit guilty because I had forgotten all about it.'

'You say this happened between half past eleven and midnight?' queried Mairin.

Ena nodded.

'As I was going out to the kitchen Mr and Mrs Callcott were just leaving. I saw them get into their carriage and drive off. Mr Hewlett and Mr Howarth were still in the dining room.

'I went outside to the kitchen and warmed the milk, and as I returned to the house and went upstairs I saw Mr Hewlett and Mr Howarth say good-night to each other on the first floor corridor. They chatted for a couple of minutes then I saw them enter their rooms.

'After that I went on down the corridor with Mrs Hewlett's glass of milk.'

'Was she all right when you entered the room?' asked Mrs Quigley.

'She told me she had enjoyed the evening.'

This was good news for James, but not for Marcus thought Mairin. Marcus' room that night was on the same floor as Mrs Hewlett.

'You ought to go to the police and tell them about this,' Mrs Quigley advised Ena. 'I don't know why you didn't do it before.'

'I never thought of it. Shall I peel those potatoes Mrs Quigley?'

'You certainly can.'

As Ena started peeling the potatoes Mairin looked at the young girl. Ena was the last person to see Mrs Hewlett alive.

9

It was getting late, so bidding them all good night Mairin went across to the house, up the back stairs to the second floor and her room.

She prepared for bed in a puzzled frame of mind, Marcus' treachery now pushed temporarily from her thoughts. First she was so happy that James was now proven innocent, but what about Ena?

Next morning she rose early and dressed, then went downstairs and across to the kitchen hut joining Mrs Quigley and Ena at the table for a simple breakfast of tea and bread and butter.

'Will you come with me to the police station in Christchurch Miss Houlihan?' asked Ena nervously. 'I don't want to go on my own. And Gilbert will have to wait outside to look after the horses.'

'Of course I will,' Mairin reassured her. 'Ena, I've suddenly thought, on that terrible morning when I went in to Mrs Hewlett's bedroom and found her dead, I didn't see an empty glass on the bedside table.'

'Mrs Hewlett asked me to wait whilst she drank it,' was Ena's simple answer.

Soon after that they set off in the family brougham, Gilbert driving. Ena was quite excited. She had never ridden in any of the family carriages before and Mairin felt she did not appreciate the seriousness of the situation.

At the police station Mairin asked for Chief Inspector MacGregor. They only had to wait a short time, and were then shown into his office. Ena told her story; Chief Inspector MacGregor appeared interested.

'This information puts a new slant on the situation. It is a great pity you did not think of coming here before to see me.'

Ena looked crestfallen.

Then the Inspector looked across at Mairin. 'But we still need more proof of innocence.'

Mairin knew what he was thinking. She could still have sneaked into Mrs Hewlett's room after Ena had left.

'I am obliged Miss for the information you have just given us. It is good news for Mr Callcott.' Then looking across at Mairin added, 'I will be in touch with your lawyer, and we will regard this visit as your weekly compulsory visit.'

They left the police station and stepped into the brougham.

'Gilbert, will you take me to my sister's,' Mairin asked as they set off. 'I have good news for her husband. I'll hire a cab for my return journey.'

A few minutes later Gilbert stopped outside Oonagh's house. Mairin bid Gilbert and Ena goodbye then walked up the path and onto the verandah of Oonagh's house. As usual Hannah was asleep in her perambulator. She knocked at the door. Oonagh opened it, and Mairin followed her into the sitting room.

'I have good news for you Oonagh. James is no longer under suspicion. Ena has just made a statement to the police.'

Mairin then related the new evidence of Ena taking Mrs Hewlett her glass of milk just before midnight and seeing Oonagh and James depart.

'That still leaves Mr Howarth in an unenviable position,' commented Oonagh. 'Didn't he stay the night?' Oonagh put her arms around her sister. 'I'm deeply sorry for what I did.'

Mairin gave her a sad smile.

'It's understandable. You were trying to protect your husband.'

'How's life these days at Worcester House whilst awaiting this dreadful trial?'

'I've been dismissed.'

'I don't understand.'

Mairin related what had happened.

Oonagh frowned. 'Is it anything to do with the book you took off the shelf?'

'I don't know,' Mairin replied in a

weary voice. 'Have you heard from James?'

'Yes. The police have not contacted him. The house is up for sale and the moment it is sold we are joining him.'

'You'll be glad when that happens.'

'I certainly will,' Oonagh replied with feeling. 'It's lonely without James.'

She picked up a gown she was making for Hannah and started sewing.

'Oonagh, who do you think murdered Mrs Hewlett?' Mairin asked at length.

'I honestly don't know. And there is insufficient grounds to convict you of the murder. I cannot see it happening. Have you given any thought to the future?'

'No. I live from day to day, and praying for a sympathetic jury.'

Oonagh walked across and touched her sister's arm.

'I'm praying as well, Mairin.'

Mairin spent the rest of the day helping Oonagh with her sewing and whilst she did so her thoughts turned to Mr Hewlett and her dismissal.

The book she had taken off the shelf had been a secret history of George III. It was a period of promiscuous behaviour of royalty. George III had had bouts of madness. Such a book would have been banned in England, and obviously not read in respectable circles.

Was it anything to do with that?

Then she remembered she had discovered a safe hidden behind the books. Was that the reason? She decided that tomorrow morning when she returned to Worcester House she would continue her investigation before Mr Hewlett returned from Kaikoura.

The following morning Mairin returned to Worcester House. Mrs Quigley and Ena were busy in the kitchen. It was brass cleaning day.

'My sister is indebted to you Ena,' Mairin told her as she joined them at the table.

Ena gave a happy smile.

'Wish I could help you Miss Houlihan.'

'I've just had a note from Miss Stuart Erskine,' Mrs Quigley informed everyone. 'Reminding me she is holding a bazaar in aid of her charity. The bazaar will be held in the grounds of Worcester House by kind permission of Mr Hewlett.

'No one said a word to me. I'm only the housekeeper. Anyway, a cart load of goods arrived this morning to be put on the stalls.'

'When is the bazaar?' asked Mairin, idly curious.

'This coming Saturday,' was the reply. 'Mr Hewlett will be back by then. Poor man, these events keep his mind occupied. He must be heartbroken. He must miss her terribly. Shame they couldn't have any children. I know he wanted a son to carry on the business.'

Mrs Quigley finished polishing the brass candlesticks. Ena put them on a tray and left the kitchen hut with them.

Mrs Quigley turned to Mairin.

'Remember the Maori odd job man? He's gone, and Aroha is very upset. Anyway, she'll get over it. I think the police ought to be told. I'm suspicious of him. Bringing in logs for a fire in this hot weather.'

'It certainly was a strange thing to do. Perhaps he is mentally unstable?' suggested Mairin.

'Not him,' Mrs Quigley was quick to reply. 'I once found some money missing from my purse, and I reckon it was him that took it.'

Aroha entered the kitchen hut. She looked as though she had been crying. Mrs Quigley gave her a sympathetic smile.

'Don't cry about him Aroha. He's not worth it. He's proved it.' Then turning to Mairin she added: 'You can stay the night if you want to Miss Houlihan. Mr Hewlett won't be back for a few more days. If we can't help each other when in need . . . '

'I'm grateful to you Mrs Quigley.'

'How are you getting on writing

those Maori stories?'

'I've almost finished them,' Mairin replied looking at Aroha. 'Do you know any more?'

Mrs Quigley laughed.

'Aroha knows hundreds. Tell Miss Houlihan another one.'

Aroha looked pleased and recounted the story of a giant called Matau who stole a beautiful girl called Manata from her father's home. It ended happily with her lover killing the giant.

Mairin quickly scribbled notes.

'Thank you Aroha,' Mairin told her. 'I must add that one to my collection.'

As Mrs Quigley had kindly offered her accommodation Mairin felt the least she could do was help with household duties, this she did for the rest of the day.

In the evening Mairin went up to her room. She could not stop thinking of the events that had led up to her dismissal. In taking that book off the shelf she had accidentally discovered the safe.

Was that the reason why Mr Hewlett had dismissed her?

As she sat there staring at the darkening landscape she began to feel it was a strong possibility. Then she started to wonder what the safe combination number could be.

Sleep was far away. There was only one thing to do and that was to go down to Mr Hewlett's study and do a little investigation. After all she had been unfairly dismissed.

She had been treated very badly.

She made her way down the stairs to the floor below, to Mr Hewlett's study. Putting the candle on the desk still wondering what the combination number could be. Mairin was in such a defiant mood that if Mr Hewlett had suddenly appeared she felt she would not have cared.

Mairin opened one of the drawers. There were letters and reports. None of the contents caught her attention. In the next drawer she found Mr Hewlett's diary.

On the first page he had written his name and address, place of birth which was some unknown village in Staffordshire. This was followed by the date of his wedding, 1861. The date had been underlined.

10

Putting the diary back in the drawer Mairin felt Mr Hewlett had underlined his wedding date because it was one of the most important dates in his life, marrying Mrs Hewlett who obviously had been the love of his life.

Her thoughts turned to Marcus. How could he have been so treacherous? Telling her he loved her. And who was this girl who came to him in the middle of the night? How had he met her? Coming to New Zealand had brought her nothing but unhappiness.

Mairin returned to her room, undressed and got into bed thinking about the safe behind the books in Mr Hewlett's study. She now felt certain the safe was the reason for her dismissal. Then again, she wondered what the safe combination number could be.

Underlining the date of his marriage, was it a reason other than an extremely important date in his life?

Suddenly she had to find out. So lighting her candle Mairin stole quietly down the stairs to the first floor where Mr Hewlett's study was situated.

Entering the room she carefully closed the door, then walked across the room and took a number of books off the shelf, placing them on the desk. The safe was now fully revealed.

The number underlined in his diary was 1861. Slowly Mairin turned the dial: 1,8,6,1. The door of the safe opened.

It was filled with Mrs Hewlett's jewellery! It was breathtaking! Diamonds, rubies, pearls, sapphires, emeralds. Mairin felt both excited and afraid. What did it mean? That Mr Hewlett had murdered his wife and then hidden her jewellery in his safe to make it look as though her jewellery had been stolen.

Suddenly she heard footsteps in the

corridor outside. She turned, frozen with fear as in the flickering light of the candle she watched the door slowly open and Mr Hewlett entered the room.

'I saw the light of the candle from the window and thought the housekeeper or butler were up to mischief. I did not think of you, you were dismissed a few days ago.'

He spoke in a quiet calm voice, then walked forward and stood a few feet from Mairin, an angry look on his face.

'I shall speak to Mrs Quigley about this. She had no right to allow you in the house.'

'Mr Hewlett, leave Mrs Quigley alone,' Mairin told him. 'She is not to blame.'

'I'm going to get the police.'

Suddenly to Mairin's astonishment, an inner strength surged through her and she wasn't afraid of this man anymore.

'You murdered your wife, then stole her jewellery to make it look like a robbery. I discovered the combination by sheer chance. If you go to the police I will tell them what you have done.'

To Mairin's surprise Mr Hewlett remained calm, then his face broke into a slow, crafty smile.

'Got more spirit than I thought. I wish my wife had been more like you. Miss Houlihan, it won't work. Chief Inspector MacGregor is a close friend of mine, and he will believe everything I tell him.'

'Explain to him why the jewellery is in your safe.'

'You put it there after you murdered my wife.'

'Me? I'm incapable of murdering her. I was very fond of her. As for the safe I only discovered it a few days ago.'

Mr Hewlett shrugged his shoulders nonchalantly.

'That is your story.'

'I had no motive to commit such a monstrous crime,' Mairin continued.

Mr Hewlett gave her a look of disbelief.

'I shall tell the Chief Inspector I had

dismissed you. I had found you unsatisfactory, so as a penniless immigrant you were desperate for money. You could not go to your brother-in-law because he had money problems of his own, and my wife had shown you where she kept the jewellery. The temptation was too great.'

'If I had done this terrible deed surely I would have run off with the jewellery and sold it.'

Mr Hewlett gave her a wry sort of smile.

'No. You are too clever for that.' Mr Hewlett started pacing the room.

'You knew the police would have a full description of the jewellery. I would have given it to them, so it would have been impossible to sell to any reputable jewellers in this country.'

He had an answer for everything. Then Mr Hewlett paused, a thoughtful expression on his face.

'I am curious to know how you discovered the combination number of the safe.'

Mairin remained silent, too embarrassed to answer the question.

'Come on Miss Houlihan, I demand an answer.'

'I found your diary and glanced through it. I was desperate to clear my name.'

'Continue,' commanded Mr Hewlett, his eyes giving her a sharp look.

'I noticed on the first page you had underlined the date of your marriage.'

Mr Hewlett pursed his lips, his eyes now had an angry look in them.

'Clever little bitch. I should have had you working for me at the bank instead of teaching my stupid wife to read and write.

'I must now decide what I must do with you until tomorrow morning when Gilbert will drive us to the police station.' He paused a moment. 'I think it best if you go back to your room for the time being.'

He opened the door, Mairin picked up her candle, and left the room with Mr Hewlett following close behind her.

In this manner they proceeded along the corridor, and up the stairs.

When they reached her room, Mairin entered, Mr Hewlett remained in the corridor and closed the door, then she heard the key turn in the lock. A moment later she heard his footsteps echoing down the corridor.

Mr Hewlett might try to murder her! If he did that would solve all his problems. Now Mairin was really afraid. Her life was truly in danger.

She went and sat on the bed. How she wished she had never come back here. She should have gone straight to Oonagh's house.

The light from the candle was now flickering. She had to escape from this house. But how? She walked across to the window. The gardens were bathed in a pale silvery light of a full moon.

She could knot the sheets together tying one to the bed leg. This Mairin attempted to do, opening the window and hanging them down the back wall of the house. Unfortunately being on the second floor she needed more sheets to reach the ground.

Mairin dressed and lay down on the bed. She had to think of something else. There was a trapdoor in the ceiling above her head. As she was on the second floor the trapdoor led into the attic which ran the length of the building. Mrs Quigley had told her about the outside staircase at the rear of the building that led up to the attic.

Here was a chance!

So putting a chair on the bed Mairin stood on it and managed to open the trapdoor. Then balancing a stool on the chair, she stood on it, gripping the edge of the trapdoor with all her strength, she gave a jump and was in the attic.

It was like a black cavern and a musty smell filled her nostrils. Feeling her way cautiously, twice she bumped into odd bits of furniture, sometimes cobwebs brushed against her face. After what seemed an eternity, she finally reached the end of the attic.

Now she had to find the door leading to the outside staircase. Mairin ran her hand along the wall feeling for the door handle. There was none. A feeling of despair swept over her. Mrs Quigley had definitely told her the outside staircase led up to the attic. There had to be a door.

For the last time Mairin ran her hand along the wall, this time slowly, with greater care. Suddenly her hand grasped a door knob. She turned it, the door opened, and a rush of cold air met her face.

Oh the joy of escaping! In the pale moonlight Mairin descended the staircase. When she reached the bottom, she crossed the yard, past the kitchen hut, now in darkness except for the inner glow from the kitchen fire, then started running down the short drive to the main road.

The road was empty, and as she walked Mairin experienced a wonderful sense of freedom. After a few miles she sat down by the roadside for a rest.

Where was she heading? It had to be Oonagh.

As Mairin approached Christchurch the first light of dawn appeared in the eastern sky. There was little traffic on the road and few people about. When she reached Oonagh's house the relief was enormous.

She entered by the back door knowing Oonagh kept the key under a plant pot, crept upstairs, along the short corridor and tapped on Oonagh's door.

'Oonagh. It's me. Mairin.'

'Come in,' came a sleepy voice.

Mairin entered the room. Oonagh stirred and opened her eyes.

'Whatever is the matter Mairin?'

There was a pause and then Mairin spoke.

'I know who murdered Mrs Hewlett!'

11

Oonagh gazed at her sister in wide eyed astonishment.

'You know who murdered Mrs Hewlett!' she exclaimed in an incredulous voice.

Mairin nodded.

'It's Mr Hewlett.'

'Mr Hewlett? It can't be.'

Mairin then related to Oonagh everything that had happened. When she had finished there was silence for a moment.

'But Mr Hewlett loved his wife,' Oonagh exclaimed. 'And had no need to rob her of her jewellery. He is a wealthy man. Everyone knows that.'

'He took her jewellery to make it look like a robbery.'

Oonagh looked amazed.

'What are you going to do now?'

'Tell the police and I must go to

Patrick O'Brien. He is my defence lawyer.'

Oonagh got out of bed and started dressing.

'Mairin, before you do anything you are going to have some breakfast. You look exhausted.'

At the breakfast table Oonagh told Mairin her latest news.

'The house has finally been sold, which now means we can pay off our debts.'

'Oonagh, why do you have debts? James had a well paid position at the bank, and you appear to lead a modest kind of life.'

Oonagh sighed.

'I suppose you had better know. I've discovered that James got mixed up with a gambling group here in Christchurch. In the evenings he wasn't working late at the bank, he was gambling.'

'A gambling group!' Mairin exclaimed amazed. 'I would never have thought it of him.'

Oonagh gave a big sigh.

'It took a hold of him, his life was out of control, and the only thing he could do was to get away from these bad companions. Leave the country, go to Australia and join his parents. Start a new life.'

They had just finished breakfast. Suddenly there was a loud hammering at the front door.

'I'll see who it is,' said Mairin as she rose from the table and hurried into the hall. Then suddenly she felt afraid. It might be Mr Hewlett. Gingerly she opened the door.

It was Marcus with Zillah, the girl she had befriended on the GEORGE WENTWORTH. Her face was badly bruised and cut. She had a black eye and her gown was torn.

Mairin's arms went around her old friend.

'So it was you Zillah who went to Marcus' house,' exclaimed Mairin, relief in her voice. Then turning to Marcus added, 'What a stupid mistake I made.'

Marcus gave her a soft smile.

'I knew I'd find you here.'

'But what happened?' asked Mairin gazing at Zillah's bruised face and torn gown.

'The man she was introduced to at the agency appeared pleasant at first,' Marcus explained. 'They went through a form of marriage service, and it was afterwards when they moved to the house at the crossroads near my sheep station that he became violent. Zillah said he appeared to enjoy beating her.

'I met her by chance a few weeks ago badly bruised walking along the lane near my house. She was very upset and told me her troubles. I told her the next time it happens she was to come to me for help. This she did.'

Marcus looked pointedly at Mairin.

'I'm so sorry so sorry . . . ' apologised Mairin, a crestfallen look on her face. 'I completely misunderstood.'

Oonagh appeared at that moment and Marcus explained the situation to her.

'Zillah is welcome to stay here until she decides what to do,' Oonagh told them.

'Thanks,' said Marcus. 'That is very kind of you.'

'Come with me Zillah,' smiled Oonagh. 'I'll take you to my house-keeper and she will show you your room.'

The two women left the entrance hall. Mairin took Marcus into the sitting room. As usual he looked strong, handsome and sunburnt, and Mairin felt a sadness in her heart.

Marcus gave her a quizzical look. 'I have just called at Worcester House. Mrs Quigley is very upset. Mr Hewlett left very early this morning, driving himself, he did not want Gilbert with him.

'You, Mairin, had disappeared. Someone had locked you in your room and you had escaped through the attic. What is going on?'

'I found a safe in his study,' Mairin explained. 'It was hidden behind his books. And by accident found the combination number. I opened the safe and it was full of Mrs Hewlett's jewellery. Then Mr Hewlett came into the room and I thought he was going to kill me. Instead he locked me in my room, and fortunately I managed to escape.' Marcus frowned, a thoughtful look on his face.

'With all the incriminating evidence his only hope would be to leave the country immediately. But how and where would he go?'

Marcus paced the room a thoughtful look on his face. Suddenly he turned.

'There is a ship, the FRANCIS NICHOLSON leaving Port Lyttelton today for Sydney. I know of this because I had been considering shipping a flock of ewes on it then changed my mind.'

'There is a chance he might be on it.' There was a note of excitement in Mairin's voice.

'I'd better tell the police immediately.' Marcus glanced at the clock on the mantelpiece.

He moved towards the door.

'Take care Mairin. Remember you are in danger. You know too much.'

Marcus left the house and from the window Mairin felt tense and worried as she watched him drive away.

'What is going on?'

Mairin turned to find Oonagh had just entered the room.

'Marcus has just gone to the police,' Mairin explained. 'There is a ship leaving Port Lyttelton today for Sydney. We think there is a possibility that Mr Hewlett might be on board.'

Oonagh gave Mairin a thoughtful look.

'Patrick O'Brien is your defence lawyer. He should be told what is happening.'

'You're right Oonagh. I'll go and see him now.'

'Take the pony and trap.'

'No thanks Oonagh. I can walk there. His house is only two streets away.'

There was a slim possibility that Mr

Hewlett might still be in Christchurch. Pushing that hideous thought from her mind, Mairin left the house and walked quickly down the street.

When she reached Patrick's house he was just about to leave for his office and invited her into his sitting room. He gave her a welcoming smile.

'Patrick, I am so sorry to trouble you but there have been new developments.'

She then proceeded to tell him everything that had happened. Patrick listened carefully then gave her a sad smile.

'Mairin, I now know where your heart lies. When you needed help you turned to Marcus Howarth, not me,' he ended in a melancholy tone.

'I'm sorry Patrick. So sorry.'

'It was not to be,' he sighed. 'Come, I'll take you back to your sister's and no doubt the moment you have any news you will keep me informed.'

All the way back to Oonagh's Mairin and Patrick sat in silence. Mairin had unwittingly caused Patrick distress, but one day he would find the right woman who would love and cherish him. She was sure.

When they reached Oonagh's house Mairin was now extremely concerned about Marcus. She said goodbye to Patrick and entered the house. It was the longest day of Mairin's life. Each minute seemed like an hour, Mairin praying that no harm would come to Marcus for if Mr Hewlett was at Port Lyttelton he might be armed.

When evening came Mairin felt her heart was going to break. What had happened? Was Marcus alive or dead? She knew with certainly now she loved him with all her heart.

Suddenly she heard a horse clip clopping up the street, followed by footsteps on the front path, then came the knocking on the door. Mairin ran to open it.

It was Marcus, alive and well, with Chief Inspector MacGregor and Sergeant MacAllister. She was overjoyed.

Mairin showed them into the sitting

room. Oonagh and Zillah joined them.

'What happened?' Mairin asked looking from one to the other.

'We went to Lyttelton and went on board the FRANCIS NICHOLSON and spoke to the captain,' Chief Inspector MacGregor informed them. 'He told us two cabins had been booked in the name of Hewlett, and just as he spoke we saw Mr Hewlett and Miss Stuart Erskine coming on board.'

'Did he have the jewellery with him?' asked Mairin.

Chief Inspector MacGregor nodded.

'We found it in his luggage. And he confessed to murdering his wife. He has been arrested and charged with the crime. The case will be heard at the Assizes in a few weeks time.

'Miss Stuart Erskine will be held on remand as a suspected accomplice. So Miss Houlihan, there will be no further need for you to report to us weekly.'

'Will I be required to give evidence at the trial?'

'You might, but purely in the capacity of the lady's companion. I'll say good evening to you. And before I go I must add that we owe Mr Howarth a debt of gratitude for knowing of the imminent departure of the FRANCIS NICHOLSON for Sydney. Otherwise we would not have made the arrest.'

The police departed, and Oonagh and Zillah left the room. Marcus turned to Mairin.

'A few hours after you left the sheep station, I received a letter from Miss Stuart Erskine informing me she was breaking off the engagement and therefore there would be no question of suing me for breach of promise. It was obvious she had met someone else.'

'Eloping with Mr Hewlett,' reflected Mairin. 'I'm still puzzled. Murdering his wife, making it look like a robbery. What an extraordinary thing to do. Mr Hewlett is one of the most respected and richest citizens in Christchurch.'

At that moment to Mairin's surprise Patrick O'Brien arrived at the house.

Oonagh showed him into the sitting room.

'I've just been to the police station and been told of the arrest of Mr Hewlett,' he told them. Then he turned to Mairin. 'After you left this morning Mairin, I felt so concerned that I went immediately to Mr Hewlett's bank, and to my astonishment was told that Mr Hewlett had just sold the bank.'

'When did he sell it?' asked Marcus amazed at this news.

'The sale was completed two days ago,' he replied.

'To whom?' Marcus asked. 'I knew nothing of this.'

'Someone who lives in Sydney, Australia. I can't recall the name at the moment, the clerk at the bank has it.'

'He thought of everything,' commented Marcus, a wry tone in his voice.

Patrick nodded in agreement.

'I have to tell you I had been suspicious of the relationship between Mr Hewlett and Miss Stuart Erskine for some time.'

'But why didn't you mention it?' Mairin asked.

'I had no proof, it was just an instinctive feeling watching the way they looked at each other.'

'As one of the wealthiest men in Christchurch,' commented Marcus, 'why didn't he just divorce Mrs Hewlett, he had the money to do it.'

Patrick shook his head.

'Miss Stuart Erskine is very religious and does not recognise divorce. She had to marry a bachelor or a widower. So it is obvious that Mr Hewlett decided to become a widower to qualify as a prospective husband, and of course make people think a robber had murdered his wife in order to steal her jewellery.'

'What a tragic business,' commented Mairin. 'But why did they have to elope?'

'I've given that some thought,' replied Patrick. 'Mr Hewlett is one of the richest men in Christchurch. Miss Stuart Erskine was hoping her parents would approve, but unfortunately it is obvious they did not. They would have discovered his background is common working class. Someone did tell me his father was a blacksmith.

'Miss Stuart Erskine's father, Brigadier General Stuart Erskine, is second cousin to Lord Stuart Erskine, so Mr Howarth as brother to a baron was regarded as a far better proposition.

'Her parents belong to the old school. In their opinion breeding is more important than money, and it is obvious that Miss Stuart Erskine regarded money as more important than breeding.

'I have to leave you now and return to my office.'

Patrick left the house and Oonagh had to go upstairs to attend to Hannah.

'Mr Hewlett engaged you Mairin, to make people think he was a kind and thoughtful husband,' commented Marcus as they moved onto the verandah.

'And murdered his wife in order to marry Miss Stuart Erskine. What men will do when they are obsessed about a woman.'

Mairin spoke in a quiet voice. The events of the past twenty four hours had deeply shocked her.

Suddenly Marcus' arms enfolded her, holding her close to him. In his eyes there was the look of a man deeply in love.

'I'm obsessed about you. I think of you morning, noon and night. Will you marry me Mairin?'

She could say yes and she would have truly gained revenge on his terrible family. But now she had no interest in revenge, she just wanted to be forever with the man she loved. Mairin's eyes filled with tears as she murmured her assent.

'I love you Marcus.'

Then his mouth came down on hers. It was the hottest, most passionate kiss she had ever received.

'You have made me a very happy man Mairin. Oh by the way, I've just had bad news from England.'

'Bad news?' exclaimed Mairin, feeling most concerned. 'What has happened?'

'My brother has been killed in a riding accident.'

No matter how angry she felt about the Howarths she had to express her condolence.

'I'm so sorry to hear this.'

'I never expected it to happen,' continued Marcus. 'He was a good rider. He loved hunting.'

Mairin gave Marcus a thoughtful look.

'Wasn't he a widower with no children?'

Marcus nodded. 'And of course it now means I inherit; title and estate.'

'Your mother heartily dislikes me. She would never welcome me into the family.' Mairin spoke in a bitter voice remembering that terrible night when she had been accused of theft and given instant dismissal.

'I've just received a letter from her. She is now a very sick woman. Oh by the way, she mentions her own personal maid stole her brooch. Mother began to be suspicious of the girl and ordered her room to be searched. The brooch was found. Forgive mother.'

'I forgive her.'

'You are a generous woman Mairin. This now means we must return to England, sell the estate, except of course mother's Dower House, then return to New Zealand to start a new life. You agree?'

'Of course I do,' Mairin replied.

Marcus grasped her hand in his as they walked down the verandah steps and into the garden.

'We are the music makers,'

he quoted softly,

'And we are the dreamers of dreams
Wandering by lone sea breakers.'

'Yet we are the movers and shakers,'

Mairin joined in,

'Of the world forever it seems.'

The sun was now setting at the western horizon, and the sky was streaked with gold.

THE END

We do hope that you have enjoyed reading this large print book.

Did you know that all of our titles are available for purchase?

We publish a wide range of high quality large print books including:
Romances, Mysteries, Classics
General Fiction
Non Fiction and Westerns

Special interest titles available in large print are:
The Little Oxford Dictionary
Music Book, Song Book
Hymn Book, Service Book

Also available from us courtesy of Oxford University Press:
Young Readers' Dictionary
(large print edition)
Young Readers' Thesaurus
(large print edition)

For further information or a free brochure, please contact us at:
Ulverscroft Large Print Books Ltd.,
The Green, Bradgate Road, Anstey,
Leicester, LE7 7FU, England.
Tel: (00 44) **0116 236 4325**
Fax: (00 44) **0116 234 0205**

*Other titles in the
Linford Romance Library:*

HER HEART'S DESIRE

Dorothy Taylor

When Beth Garland's great aunt Emily dies, she leaves Greg, her boyfriend, in Manchester — along with her successful advertising job — to return to live in Emily's cottage. Feeling disillusioned with Greg and his high-handed attitude, she finds herself more and more attracted to her aunt's gardener, Noah. But Noah seems to be hiding from the past, whilst Greg has his own ideas about the direction of their relationship. Surrounded by secrecy and deceit, how will Beth ever find true love?

PRECIOUS MOMENTS

June Gadsby

The heartbreak was all behind her, but hearing her name mentioned on the radio, and that song — their special song — brought bittersweet memories rushing back through the years. It had to be a coincidence, and was best forgotten — but then Lara opened the door to find her past standing there. The moment of truth she had dreaded for years had finally arrived, and she wasn't sure how to handle it . . .

THE SECRET OF SHEARWATER

Diney Delancey

When Zoe Carson inherits a cottage in Cornwall, she takes a holiday from her job in London to stay at the cottage. There, she makes friends with the local people, including the hot-tempered Gregory Enodoc. Zoe is glad of their friendship when events take a sinister turn and the police become involved. And when she decides to leave London to live permanently at the cottage, Zoe is unaware of the dangers into which this will lead her . . .

SWEET CHALLENGE

Joyce Johnson

London life for Chloe Duncan is changed forever when she accepts an invitation to visit her previously unknown Scottish great aunt, Flora Duncan. Chloe loves the peace and beauty of rural Highland life at Flora's croft, but mysteries and tensions in her great aunt's past disturb this tranquillity. Land disputes involve her in danger and, whilst unravelling the mystery of Flora's lost love, Chloe's own heart is jeopardised when she meets handsome New Zealander Steve McGlarran . . .